Father Meme

FATHER MEME

Gerald Vizenor

UNIVERSITY OF NEW MEXICO PRESS

ALBUQUERQUE

13 12 11 10 09 08   1 2 3 4 5 6

Library of Congress Cataloging-in-Publication Data

Vizenor, Gerald Robert, 1934–
Father Meme / Gerald Vizenor.
     p. cm.
     ISBN 978-0-8263-4515-8 (alk. paper)
1. Ojibwa Indians—Fiction.
2. Child sexual abuse by clergy—Fiction.
3. Acolytes—Fiction. 4. Revenge—Fiction.
5. Minnesota—Fiction. I. Title.
     PS3572.I9F38 2008
     813'.54—dc22

                 2008015029

Designed and typeset by Mina Yamashita
Composed in Adobe Garamond Pro, bringing together elements
of Claude Garamond's Garamond and Robert Granjon's Granjon
in a contemporary typeface by Robert Slimbach.
Display composed in Frutiger 77 Black Condensed,
designed by Adrian Frutiger in 1976.
Printed by Thomson-Shore, Inc. on 55# Natures Natural.

In Memory of Dane White

Maybe we don't love life enough? Have you noticed that death alone awakens our feelings? How we love the friends who have just left us? How we admire those of our teachers who have ceased to speak, their mouths filled with earth! Then the expression of admiration springs forth naturally, that admiration they were perhaps expecting from us all their lives. But do you know why we are always more just and more generous toward the dead? The reason is simple. With them there is no obligation. They leave us free and we can take our time, fit the testimonial in between a cocktail party and a nice little mistress, in our spare time, in short.

—Albert Camus, *The Fall*

Contents

Mayagi Ashandiwin:
Strange, Exotic, Commodity Foods
1

Giiwanaadingwaam:
Bad Dreams, Nightmares
13

Naniizaanizi Gakiiwe:
Dangerous Portage
37

Bagidenjige:
Release Thoughts, Hold a Funeral
85

Mayagi Ashandiwin

Please excuse my intrusion, *madame*, but are you by chance dining alone tonight? I ask only because this is the best table in the restaurant to see the sunset, a spectacular sight at this time of the year. The very hues are traces of creation, as you can see, and waver on the horizon. The marvelous breaks of light touch the heart and inspire poetry. There, across the bay, the mighty red pines bow to each other, always to each other, grateful by seasons and ready to dance in the dash and remains of light, light, light.

I presume you are not here to gamble. Truly, your hands are so gentle, such lovely, nimble fingers, apparently not toned to the tedious motion of slot machines, and your eyes are honest, much too generous to feign a hand of poker. Forgive my gaze, *madame*, but my compliments are not the mere cause of flattery. Casinos, you might say, enervate the mind and weaken the heart and hands, the very ruins of native sense, vision, and sovereignty, but this is a four stars restaurant, a natural reason to drive more than a hundred miles for dinner on the reservation. Rightly so, the attribution of four stars is rather curious if not exceptional. The *Michelin Guide* awards one to three stars. The Canoe Rib Voyageur, *waaginaa*, a new tourist enterprise, created four stars for native casino restaurants.

My apologies for being so eager, as you rightly notice, but perhaps you would allow me to translate the menu, as the principal chef decided to use native words for the entrées. The customers seem to appreciate the exotic custom, and they learn a few words of *anishinaabe* at the same time.

Chippewa, you are correct, *madame*, is the name of the *anishinaabe* in English. The dictionary name, as you know, is an uncertain transcription, a simulation, that comes to natives by way of an empire nomination. American Indian is another dominion simulation. I use the word *native* in my stories. English is obsessed with empire sanctions, a language of simulations, transitive tenets, and cultural impunities, and the very dominance of ordinary dictionaries makes it very difficult to otherwise evince a native word from the empire nominations. There, you have my titular lecture. Yes, you are doubly correct, my singular choice and reign of words is precise, a tribute to natural reason.

Thank you, *madame*, for inviting me to join you for dinner. The waiters know me here, as you can see, and they treat me with deference, a certain tease of distinction, savoir faire, or, you might say, native familiarity. I sit at this very table three or four times a week to move with the sunset, meet visitors to the casino, strangers to the *anishinaabe* menu, and pursue my stories about this chancy parvenu reservation, but never on weekends.

The restaurant, you see, is overrun by seasons of hunters in designer camouflage, snowmobilers in noisy insulated suits, men and women of sport and mockery, the sounds of wild weekenders. Shrewdly, the casino manager corners these holiday hunters, preys on their sentiments of chance, animal, fowl, and material fatigue, and that, *madame*, covers the actual cost of this exotic restaurant.

Thank you, the waiters know exactly my tastes and what to concoct for me. Hendrick's Gin over clear, thick slivers of ice, tonic, and a slice of cucumber, always. My curious customs create a sense of presence, a singular native presence in the midst of situational losers at the casino, and the comeback stories are memorable. Haute Médoc Red Bordeaux for *madame*, a wine of cultural tributes, and for me a distinctive gin infused with Bulgarian Rose. I am a habitué, as you might imagine, of the Mayagi Ashandiwin Casino Restaurant.

A toast to your good health, my friend, and may we share memorable stories over dinner. Yes, the waiters are curious about our conversation. They notice our eyes and hands; already we are laughing as friends. You are very sensible to wonder about my countenance and conventions. Yes, my shirts are custom tailored by Turnbull and Asser on Jermyn Street in London. I see you wear silk and linen, natural and worldly. Yet, *madame*, we are surrounded by mundane synthetics. Decadence, would you agree, is a pretentious, weary indulgence, not the mere distance of paucity and tailored clothes. My taste for distinctive clothes came very slowly, as you can imagine, starting on the reservation with only one flannel shirt at a time, and two pair of thick socks, the incredible conversion of a threadbare altar boy to a cosmopolitan journalist. I retired a few years ago and built a cabin near the mission, eight times larger than the one my father built more than sixty years ago. I have solar panels now; we had plastic sheets over the windows then.

You bear my intrusive manner with humor, but my way is not the same every night, and certainly this is not my needy side. I eat alone at least once a week, at this very table, but not by choice. The nightly diners, even at the sunset window, are not always a pleasant chance. Stray hunters invade the restaurant once or twice a week. They loudly toast and boast, and propagate the cruel separation of humans and animals, never storiers of natural reason. The hunters are poseurs in bulky camouflage, and they have no tragic wisdom or sense of irony. A hunter without irony is a monotheist by dominion, crosier in hand, and, without a trace of mortality or grace, almost dead at the Stations of the Cross. Dylan Thomas comes to mind, *madame*, the turns of ironic mercy in one of his poems, Death shall have no dominion. The devotion is recast, in part, from Romans, Knowing as we do that Christ, once raised from the dead, is never to die again. He is no longer under the dominion of death.

You must be familiar, then, with the history of the woodland fur trade? The French and *anishinaabe* were rapacious trappers, hunters, carnal woodland lovers, of course, and brought the otter, beaver, muskrat, martin, and other animals close to an unnatural extinction. Would you agree, the fur trade was a crime of genocide? Yes, of course, monotheistic, species genocide. The Chinese silk trade, a mere turn to silkworm fashions, saved the beaver from extinction, and by irony. Severe, indeed, *madame*, and the fur trade names of the waiters are an ironic appeasement for that genocide, the traces of breath, heart, and memory of woodland animals.

The waiters, as you can see, are dressed for the postmodern trade, or at least the notions of métis culture. The waistbands and hats are jaunty, couture. The waiters were actually trained for a few weeks at a tourist restaurant in Paris. They have assumed old trade names, once a practice of natives at the fur posts because their nicknames were uncommon and outsiders could not easily pronounce or transcribe the sounds. Michel Cadotte is our waiter, and even the women take the names of male traders. Peter Vezina, over there, she tends the bar. Basile Hudon dit Beaulieu is the maître d'hôtel who seated you at my sunset window. She was a lecturer in anthropology at the university for many years but decided there were more distinctive characters on the reservation, at the Good Cheer Casino, and at the Mayagi Ashandiwin Restaurant.

True, the salaries are much better at the restaurant than at the university, and you are very perceptive to suggest that some women writers assume a masculine nom de plume to find a publisher, and nuns once espoused the names of men, the saints, an unbearable, ironic collusion of monotheistic and matrimonial servitude to Jesus Christ. Surely, *madame*, you would agree, and inquire with me, Who were the ring bearers in such a perverse crusade?

Please accept my apologies for that profuse and rather insistent, cryptic irony. I would not want to abuse or depreciate your religious sentiments or signatures. The fur trade, you see, was at the verge of a new world of monotheistic contravention, derision, greed, and animal genocide. The state mandated the fashion economy of the fur trade, and church missions were wicked conspirators in the separation, dominance, and animal genocide. Native communities have never been the same for the ratty priests sent to convert natives on reservations. I was an altar boy for a wicked mission priest. Since then, *madame*, the creators hear more irony in my censure of the Roman Catholic Church.

Catholic schools? Really? Now that is a severe, disciplinary education that never ends. Perhaps you are a lawyer because of the strict reign of parochial schools. My dubious tuition was at a mission church on the reservation. Severe, to be sure, and the pedagogy was a nightmare. I was an altar boy, now a server, for a wicked priest on the reservation. Not far from here, near Wiindigoo Lake. Father Meme was a depraved and loathsome mission priest. We gave him the nickname *meme*, a red headed woodpecker in *anishinaabe*, because of his bright mound of red hair, not the meme of culture or biology.

How would you respond to the abuses, the actual curses of sleazy priests? My mother and a few tricky elders told me to respect the mission, honor the priests, and, by the secrecy of confessions, bear the burdens of penitence, and forgive the abuses of others, especially priests. Father Meme, however, was truly an evil presence with rosy cheeks, a cold and nasty bleeder. He abused the altar boys and our ancestors buried near the mission. That priest was cursed by ravens and might have brought down the mercy of the church by his confessions. He was sacrificed, the common justice of natural reason, not forgiven. Only the actual sacrifice of that priest is forgivable.

I am relieved, frankly, that you are no longer persuaded by the patriarchs and hierarchy of the church. I am doubly pleased because your censure of the priests invites me to be more descriptive and demonstrative in my stories about the depravity of priests on the reservation. Father Meme raped the other altar boys, Pants and Bear.

I am curious, of course, and must ask what brings you to the reservation? The Good Cheer Casino and, of course, the exotic menu at the Mayagi Ashandiwin Restaurant. Actually, the best reason is to see the great rush of sunsets over Leech Lake. Michel Cadotte, our waiter, told me you are a lawyer and historian from France.

Chippewa Constitution? Now that, *ma chère madame*, is very unusual, an extraordinary reason to travel thousands of miles to inquire about native rights and sovereignty. Native rights by birth, blood, breach, and bane, the alliteration of bigotry. I appreciate your dedication to consider mixed race natives, or crossbloods, and the racial enticements of separatism by the federal government. Some treaties were written that way but never endorsed. Cherokee separatism, of course, and by historical comparison the blood quantum provisions of other tribal constitutions. Yes, there were similar sentiments here, moves to separate the cross-bloods from tribal citizenship, but the racial notions of federal agents have not been taken seriously. The Cherokee, as you know, were slavers, and then, five or six generations later they voted to deny the rights to almost three thousand freedmen, but racial separatism is never exoneration for the shame of slavery. The Cherokee divvied up the race and tone of relatives, the brotherly hues of war and wedlock. Now we hear the casino blues of native slavers in the ruins of servitude and the Confederacy. The Cherokee once benefited from the labor, culture, and color of their slaves, a wicked legacy. The recent plebiscite of racial separatism was motivated by greed, dominance, and racial hatred.

Pedigree separatism is not a practice of native sovereignty and should never represent natural reason or the common interests of native cultures and survivance.

You are absolutely right, *madame*, the *anishinaabe* have never been slavers. The French fur trade was the primary source of our cultural union with outsiders and empires, and the *anishinaabe* were loyal to the Union in the Civil War. Now, any bloodthirsty separatist referenda might exclude the entire tribe by skin hues and strains of progenitor bounty. The government on this reservation, however, proscribes the use of the word *race*, the cruel arithmetic quantum of bloody genes, to determine the presence and rightful residence of native citizens.

The narrator in *The Fall*, a novel by your esteemed compatriot Albert Camus, inquired if it might be better for those who cannot do without slaves to nominate them free men? The point of the query is a good conscience, and that is certainly ironic. Natives were never the best slaves, and so they would never be freedmen. Native rights would always be the ironic strain of sovereignty. Would you agree that past slaves and freedmen are owed compensation?

Leech Lake shimmers by slants of curious light, the eternal motion of waves, waves, waves. Look, the sun bounces over the bay. You can see the everlasting blaze of sunsets every autumn night from this very window. The air is clear, clean, and bright, more inspired by the sudden, cold turn of seasons. There, near the dock, the ravens march on the shoreline and catch the common shine of our ancestors. We catch the sun, and the same dance of light that rouses the ravens, red pine, and birch wavers in your red wine, and there, brightly in the slivers of magical ice in my gin.

Do you sense the abiding melancholy of the sunset? The first emotive states of creation, the mental conditions of animals, birds, and humans come to this moment on the horizon. We share the sunsets forever with our ancestors. The waves shimmer and bear evermore the ancestral wounds of natives, the wounds caused by the fur trade, the duplicity of federal agents and priestly missions. See, my hands hold this late sun, and my heart is almost healed by the last traces of the day. The bloody horizon gathers the memories of the night.

I promised you, *madame*, a translation of the menu before dark. You must be hungry after a long drive from the city. So, start at the top of the menu, and repeat after me. Not really, only a gentle tease. I am not a native speaker of *anishinaabemowin*, the language of the *anishinaabe*, but the words, tags, and phrases are eternal traces to that marvelous league of nature, natives, and nations. There, the first word, *miijun*, or food, is rather ordinary on the reservation, but exotic to outsiders because the *giigoonh*, fish, *mayagi bine*, pheasant, and other prosaic entrées on the menu are wild, fresh from the woodland border lakes. Yes, you are very perceptive, *mayagi* means exotic or foreign, as in the name of the restaurant and the novel preparation of the entrées, and *bine* is the word for partridge. So, the pheasant is an exotic partridge from the Old World. Yes, the fish and fowl are always fresh, caught or raised, and sometimes by native songs, in the northern woodland and lakes. The entrées are never frozen, and for that obvious reason the menu is printed for the day.

Pierre Hertel de Beaubassin, the principal chef, has personal contacts with natives who provide fresh *ogaa*, walleye, and *ginoozhe*, northern pike, from Lake Namakan, rainbow smelt in the spring, and *adikameg*, whitefish, from Chequamegon Bay in Lake Superior. Pierre is not explicitly connected to the fur trade. Rather, he selected a nom de guerre, the distinguished name of an eighteenth century French Commander at La Pointe on Madeline Island, Wisconsin.

Pierre, then, is the *mayagi* chef, and the preparations of his entrées are made even more exotic by the sauces and condiments. Really, you would like me to order? *Madame*, your tastes are exotic. I would, however, rather describe my favorite entrées, and then you can decide on one or more. So, my favorite in the autumn is *miinan mayagi bine*, or blue pheasant. Pierre roasts the pheasant with wild blueberries and serves the blue breast on a mound of *manoomin*, wild rice. The color is peculiar, to be sure, but natural, the sea, sky, and jays. Some of my friends find this tender, *nookiz*, blue breast of pheasant closer to an abstract expressionist painting than to a native dinner.

You might enjoy *akakanzhebwe waabooz*, a snowshoe hare, actually a baby rabbit, braised and stuffed with the heart and other organs, and then seasoned with *bagaani bimide*, peanut butter, *zhigaagawanzh*, onion, and *wiisagi jiisens*, or radish. Yes, *lapin de garenne*, wild, baby rabbits gently caught by natives every other day near Waboose Bay. The word *zhigaagawanzh* is related to *zhigaag*, skunk, and the name Chicago. The *waaboozwaaboo*, rabbit soup, is seasoned with peanut butter, radish, and *gichi aniibiish*, or cabbage. The word *gichi* means great, and *aniibiish* means leaf, or a great leafy vegetable. And the word *bagaani* means nut or peanut, and *bimide*, oil or grease.

So, are you with me for the next entrée on the menu? Another favorite of mine is the fish soup, *giigoonhwaaboo*, seasoned with *mishiimin*, apple, *giikanaamozigan*, bacon, *mandaamin*, corn, *bagesaan*, plum, yes plum, and *okaadaak*, carrot, *ookwemin*, black cherry, *manoominaaboo*, wild rice broth, and, at last, *giizhik*, white cedar ashes. Believe me, that is a very tasty fish soup. You might start with a small bowl. Basile, the maître d'hôtel, boasts that the fish soup cures nausea and seasickness. Pierre, the chef, naturally has the last word. Here, at the end of the menu, above his signature, he wrote *bakadekaazo*, the *anishinaabe* word means, to pretend to be hungry.

Giiwanaadingwaam

The Good Cheer Casino was the inspiration of a native poet who borrowed the name from one of your revered countrymen, Samuel de Champlain, the sturdy seventeenth century navigator and soldier in Acadia, New France. Champlain founded the Ordre de Bon Temps to promote good health, humor, and the favor of hunters. By turns the soldiers competed with each other to provide fresh meat and fish for the colony. The daily meals became natural ceremonies of good cheer. The colony survived the severe winters by worthy rivalry, the ritual bouts, natural heats of hunters, and by many festive events. Four centuries later, as you can see, the elected leaders of the reservation founded the casino in the name of good cheer, an image created by a native poet. I actually know the poem by heart.

my nature
by cedar
rides on the wind
good cheer
good cheer
good cheer
never in silence
the ravens
tease the sunrise
seasons of chance
our nature

Heather Misko, the most distinguished poet on the reservation, is forever honored at the casino. Three roulette tables bear her name, the Misko Wheels. I am not a machine gambler, but those who are testify that their luck seems to improve by reciting poems as the wheel turns. The chances are better with the recitation of entire poems. Only the lines, Good cheer, Good cheer, Good cheer, are not enough apparently to win on the Misko Wheels.

Pierre would be gratified to know that you wiped the plate clean with *zaasakokwaan*, his special fry bread. This is not the usual hydrogenated fried white bread that clogs the heart, a grievous legacy of colonial mission fare. Here the grains are whole and baked in olive oil, a new native focaccia. Yes, you are right, the pronunciation of some *anishinaabe* words is hard to remember. I am not a native speaker, as you know, but the distinctive sounds of the words, and my facility with the menu, creates for me a sense of a native presence. I actually feel secure in the mere sound of the language.

Naturally, you would ask me about the dubious turns and tributes of the American Indian Movement. Really, your interest is no surprise. Americans, and the French, in particular, are too easily swayed by wannabe shamans, and by the many poses of native warriors. Yes, some of the urban warriors dress to the tribal nines for their sponsors in Paris, Rome, Los Angeles, San Francisco, and, of course, Santa Fe, New Mexico. Do you want me to continue? Right, but this is not a friendly subject to discuss at the end of a fine dinner, actually not a suitable gist over any meal, fast food or otherwise.

Your sentiments, *madame*, are admirable but regrettably romantic. So many of the poseur warriors are criminals and cultural squanderers. The French never tolerated such romantic notions of resistance in their colonies. Americans, however, actually promoted courses in native spirituality at state and federal prisons, far removed from the sources of the mighty visionaries. I mistrust the sentiments that would honor criminals as spiritual mentors, native mediators of traditions, culture, or sovereignty.

Some of the militants in the movement are as depraved as prurient priests. Do you frown to denounce the poseurs or the priests? Surely you would not overlook the wicked credos of wannabe warriors and abusers of children in the many costumes of authority? Criminals, federal agents, priests, and mushy militants are seldom worthy representatives of natives on reservations. Most natives turn against such romantic coercion for those very reasons. Truly detestable that some militants pose as *ogichidaa*, a warrior or ceremonial leader, but their tutelage is common, mundane, more institutional than spiritual, an imitation, and seldom, if ever, inspired by the native guidance of the *anishinaabe midewiwin*, the Grand Medicine Society.

Who? Clyde Bellecourt, to name only one militant, is an easy choice. He was a malefactor, a criminal, not an honorable native warrior or healer. You seem shocked by my impeachment of the man. Listen, he was convicted in federal court for drug crimes. There is nothing romantic about the distribution and use of addictive narcotics. Surely, *madame*, someone by bother or irony has already founded Groupe de Soutien à Clyde Bellecourt in Paris. Yes, it would be wise to change the subject. And yet you ask me why? Simply because so many of the leaders in the movement are corrupt, scandalous, and those stories have never been a good digestive. Dishonor and dishonesty have never been a native contingency, and besides, leftist radicals around the world use the movement merely to denounce the United States. So, who are these poseurs? Dennis Banks has become an organic wild rice merchant, and he is no stranger at the casinos. You disagree with my critique? Naturally, you should, but that does not mean your nation is the only enlightened arbiter of resistance, reservation politics, and native liberté.

Look, only the faint traces of color on the horizon, and the boat lights glint on the black water. The Fourth of July celebrations are spectacular on Walker Bay. Hundreds of boats gather silently in the dark. Many, many whispers float ashore, and a sense of community grows by the sounds. Then, the mighty burst of fireworks, rockets launched into the sky, a great explosion of transient light over the bay. The bright streamers, red, white, and blue, reach over the boats. Faces brighten on the dock. The colors crack and shatter overhead, and the silent shine is carried on the magical water. The light survives on the slightest waves and is folded forever with the whispers into the currents of Leech Lake.

The casino might honor you one summer night with a boat parade and celebration of Bastille Day. Truly, *madame*, you should inform the tribal government of the observance when you inquire about the Chippewa Constitution. Some of the old men are sentimental about the old cultures of the Great Lakes and New France. The fur trade is a shared native legacy, and most of our surnames are French. The *anishinaabe* bear a memorable, cultural, and historical association, and a blood right to celebrate the same colors, the Stars and Stripes on the Fourth of July, and *le drapeau tricolore* on Bastille Day.

Father Meme once reached out to hold my hand just as the bright colors of the Stars and Stripes burst overhead near the city dock. He pretended to be patriotic. I was twelve years old at the time and remember my severe confusion, the spectacular, warm, humid summer night, faces alight, the fireworks overhead, and his cold, greedy hand over mine. That was the first time he ever touched me, but not the last. I learned later that he had already sexually abused two other altar boys on the reservation. Truly, everything Father Meme touched, sacred objects, bodies, books, bells, mission rails, doors, chairs, and the chalice, held a trace of his cold, cold hands. His touch was wintry. Pants and Bear, my best friends, the other altar boys, were convinced the priest could freeze water with his finger. That pinkish, fleshy man never perspired, and yet the scent of his body, the sacramental wine, cedar, and winter rose bath salts, permeated the mission church. The old men on the reservation told stories about the priest that he could cool a wood fire, ice the humor of a child with an evil eye, and that his pungent priestly scent was treacherous. The librarian at the school said she sensed his cold touch on the books. I could actually feel his chilly presence at a distance. Yes, he could be friendly, and at times even rather shy. Some natives were distracted by his wide grin, the cold, perfect shine of his huge teeth could charm the devil.

You are very generous to ask about native nicknames and my family. Most natives have at least one nickname, and some of the names are ironic. I was three years old when my parents moved to the city. My father found occasional work as a truck driver, but the union threatened scabs, and only a few months later my father was murdered. Shelter, my mother, returned with me to the reservation. Who would care for a native widow and her son in the city?

The first memory of my father is in a cold basement in the city. There were no basements on the reservation, so that alone was memorable. This is my true remembrance, no one else has ever told me this story. Do you trust those storiers who create their memories? How would you know the verity of memory?

Crier, my father, held my hand as we walked down the stairs and told me to choose a puppy from a litter of six in the corner. The noisy puppies were stacked together, nursing and kneading each other. I could not decide, and turned to my father. Just then a brown and white mongrel raised his head and sneezed. Naturally, he was my choice, and that became his name, *jaachaamo*, or Sneeze. My father was dead a few weeks later. He left me with a personal memory and my first dog. Sneeze was a healer, a shaman of the native sneeze, and he was at my side every day on the reservation for thirteen years. He barked only at outsiders, strangers, and priests, never at ravens or wolves.

Nicknames, *madame*, are not always obvious. Yes, Crier is an ironic name. My father was rather shy, and he barely raised his voice even when he was scared. Crier was a tease, a nickname that might have provoked him to shout. My father was quiet, a very gentle speaker, intimate, word by word, his voice almost shadows of words, and the name remained an irony. Shelter, my mother, was so named by her grandmother, but the nickname stories were never the same. Shelter, because my mother was scared by thunderstorms, or, by her generosity and kindness, for she was an absolute shelter for the elders. My story of her nickname is that she always dreamed of owning her own house, even as a child she drew pictures of houses. My father collected materials over the years from various construction sites and from razed properties in nearby towns, and built a cabin for my mother on a natural rise near Wiindigoo Lake. Crier worked slowly because of his weak lungs and heart, the reason he was not drafted for military service. The window holes were covered with thick plastic for many, many years. No, *madame*, my experience was not tragic poverty. You see, my parents were truly in love with each other. I learned about my poverty much later at the university.

Natives favor nicknames, some descriptive, sacred, ironic, and names always have a story. Gorgeous, my great uncle, charmed women for more than fifty years with the love songs he learned in France at the end of the First World War. Pants, my best friend, once wore tight giveaway trousers, and his butt burst the seams. There was no way a native could assume or even change a nickname. Others create the stories of nicknames, and some natives have more than one name. Bear has a blunt nose, huge hands, and he was the first of my friends to show pubic hair. A single pubic hair was a significant rite of passage at the time, and worthy of a nickname.

Native nicknames are congenial conversions, creative stories of the personal experiences of compatriots, the tease and irony of dote, fancy, and amity. Family nicknames arise by chance and by the truth of observations. Children sometimes earn nicknames by their early perceptions and spontaneous manner. Only a fool would bargain for a better nickname. You, *ma chère compatriote*, will surely acquire at least one nickname if you stay on the reservation for more than a few days.

Gorgeous, as you observed, clearly encouraged our treacherous strategies to drive the priest back to the dubious healers, the Servants of the Paraclete in New Mexico. Sneeze barked many times at Mass, and the confessional, and chased the priest through the snow to his fish house, but never closed that secure distance. Sneeze was born to chase priests. Pants and Bear conspired with me to menace and renounce by deadly tricks the wicked priest. Yes, indeed, you must doubt my story of sacrifice, but you need only inquire on the reservation if the priest vanished that winter. He was last seen in the fish house, his last cathedral see.

Father Meme is dead, deservedly beaten and pushed under the ice, but if he were here tonight in the restaurant, or even in the casino, you would shiver by his presence and reach for a sweater. His name turns me cold, and his wintry touch would remain overnight on the slot machines. My ears, nose, and cheeks turned cold by his mere presence on a warm summer day, and when he touched me at the altar the cold print of his hand lingered like an obscene shadow on my shoulder. My surplice was always cold, and slightly musty, as if the priest had fondled it overnight. Sometimes his face seemed to shiver, cold and baleful, mostly when he was worried about our tricks. The pink hues of his face flushed, bright red blotches spread across his chin and forehead, and then, predictably, his nose would bleed. The confessional was always bloody. I was, to be sure, an altar boy conspirator of sacrifice. You know, *madame*, we were terrified at first, fearful that the priest would curse our families, but then we learned how to torment the priest. Nishiwe, the old man who lived near the lake, taught me how to be a sniper. The altar boys became the archenemies, the nemeses of the priest. We tormented him for three weeks, and then, late one winter night at the fish house see, we beat the priest to death with beaver and lilac coup sticks.

Gorgeous was worried about the priest, convinced that he was a winter cannibal, a *wiindigoo* monster with red bushy hair. You would be uneasy too, because the monster eats bits and pieces of humans in the winter. There is nothing, *madame*, to fear in the summer. The altar boys were duly warned that the priest was a *wiindigoo* cannibal. Gorgeous told me a traditional story about *nookomis*, the grandmother of *naanabozho*, the native trickster. The distant land he intended to visit was infested with many demons and cannibals, some of them even worse than the priest. I have never forgotten my sense of fear at the time, as my great uncle related the story of the mighty evil gambler, a monster who lives out of reach in a world without light and who has never been beaten at any game. The trickster, however, was adventurous and was determined to outwit the gambler at the native dish game, the four figures or ages of man. The trickster would wager his life and the future of the *anishinaabe* people. The trickster whistled and teased the wind as the gambler struck the dish on the ground. The four figures were not standing, not one. The evil gambler had lost the first round of the game, but there are many more games to play. Father Meme was our wicked gambler, he lost the game and was sacrificed in the fish house. Do you think that would be a good story for children?

Please imagine a narrow path that once encircled our cabin and then trailed down to the mission church and Wiindigoo Lake. That path, *madame*, now worn to the bones of memory, was my first sense of liberty. Pants and Bear invited me to be an altar boy, and the priest agreed after he took me to the fireworks. Altar boys were paid ten cents for the priestly duties, services, funerals, and weddings. I was the youngest altar boy, and that obligated me to carry, robe, and disrobe the vestments of the priest. My mother needed even the few dimes for my weekly service in a surplice because she could not find work on the reservation. I was an only child, and my mother was lonesome. My mother cried at night. I could hear her unsteady breath in the bedroom. I slept near the stove in the kitchen of our tiny cabin. Sneeze was always at my side. Native men abused my mother, the priest abused me, and together we tried to smile on the holidays.

Father Meme abused my heart, mostly, and he is the cause of my most unbearable stories. He menaced my peace on that path near home, and he even abused the memories of my ancestors. Late one night that unrighteous priest removed and burned the old wooden markers on native graves at the side of the mission church. Sneeze rushed outside and barked at the priest. My mother tried to save the markers, but the names were in flames. Luckily, most families could remember the true graves of their ancestors and set new markers with names in bright, bold letters. Father Meme declared that the markers were over pagan graves. Confessions, nosebleeds, and the ceremonies continued, but after the fire only a few older women attended services at the mission church. His winter breath haunted me and the other altar boys, and his ominous presence gave new meaning to the name of Wiindigoo Lake. You might wonder if my stories of the priest are incredible, much too extreme to be believable. I wonder myself if this was truly my experience. Do you think a person could imagine these stories?

Yes, *madame*, you understand as a lawyer how my narratives have become a vindication, the actual safeguards of my unbearable memories. Only the sacrifice of the priest saved me from suicide. Now, imagine how many children are dead by the abuse of priests and the church, dead by suicide, and the vindication stories of many, many altar boys have never been heard or remembered in stories.

Father Meme was the bane of the reservation of my birth by his wintry benedictions. So, we returned the torment and sacrificed him on the ice, but you can still sense his presence, the trace of his body at every turn on the path, and his cold, wicked touch in every crack and corner of the mission church. Father Conan Whitty, our wicked Meme, told the parishioners different stories about his family. Once he was an only child born in Fall River, Massachusetts, and ordained in the Benedictine Order. Otherwise he was an orphan, raised by immigrants from Ireland. His ancestors probably stole land from natives, and on our reservation, lonesome, orphaned, or related, he never once lived by the Rule of Saint Benedict.

Would you like more coffee? Please, two more cappuccinos, and an order of maple cookies. I know you refused dessert, but you must try pure maple. Pierre invented this dessert, but we pretend that his oatmeal, wild rice, and maple sugar cookie is an *anishinaabe* tradition. The waiters are convinced, and why not? The waiters are even more curious about your presence, our conversation, and my stories. Rightly so, they are always on the lookout for hearsay. You are very kindhearted, *madame*, to listen to my wild and violent experiences as an altar boy. Your emotive, sensitive expressions only encourage me to share more of my stories.

I retired as a journalist, after more than thirty years, and many of my close friends, judges, lawyers, novelists, professors, politicians visit me for dinner here, on their way to summer cabins. Naturally, the waiters are eager to eavesdrop on my conversations. Some of them have heard stories about the nasty priest, if only that he vanished one winter night. No crime was ever reported, and the priest was so hated that no one ever investigated his disappearance. I told my mother that he evaporated that night, but she heard some of the stories of how the altar boys teased the priest out of his perverse desires. Gorgeous actually encouraged our conspiracies, and it was his idea to construct *papier mâché* Stations of the Cross. He even convinced my grandmother to tailor castaway clothes for the altar boys to mock the bright frilly uniforms of the Swiss Guards at Vatican City.

Father Meme rented a fish house on Wiindigoo Lake. One snowy night we mounted huge paper figures around the house, fourteen grotesque, hairy red faces of the priest. Each figure had a giant, distorted penis. The priest was obsessed with that fish house, so we knew he would visit late at night. The fish house had just been towed onto the lake. We waited in a snow bank at a distance. The lake ice cracked, a blue thunder in the light of the moon. Sneeze was very excited by the winter masque. First, the black priest shuddered, turned in circles on the ice, and pounded his red bushy hair with both hands. His monster breath turned to ice, the rime of evil, and was shrouded in clouds of ice crystals. Then he marched around the figures, shouted our frosty names, and severed the paper heads. He stacked and burned the bodies near shore. I could see his wicked grin by the blue light of the flames. Sneeze chased the priest, at an escape distance, around the fish house see.

Please forgive my explicit depiction, *madame*, but the priest actually masturbated night after night over the ice hole in the fish house. The altar boys were invited many times to visit the fish house, but we were obviously constrained by the creepy manner of the priest. Father Meme always removed his clothes, and his naked body turned hoary. He was aroused by the cold, and most of the time he leaned over the ice hole. Clearly he was not a fisherman. He assured us that the fish house was a cathedral see, and we should bear his prurient touch as sacred by authority of the bishop. Yes, he was that depraved, and there is much, much more to this story. He was so hated on the reservation that even his name vanished from the official records at Saint John's Abbey, the Benedictine Monastery, and the Vatican City.

Father Meme arrived that early summer with a nosebleed, a leather suitcase, and a grocery bag of books. A few days later a huge copper bathtub was delivered to the mission church. I know it is hard to believe, but he carried hand towels to soak up the blood from his nose. Straight away he warned the altar boys that his nosebleeds were common, once or twice a week at peculiar moments. One of my duties as the new altar boy was to wash his thick blood from the floor of the confessional. Father Meme had nosebleeds, we learned later, when he was cornered at social events, and when he strained to listen to a native elder or a woman. He pulled at the bushy red hair near his ears, averted his eyes, and then blood ran down his lips into his mouth. Later he dumped the blood soaked towels in the outside toilet. Pants told stories at school about the giant, bloody flies that survived the winter in the mission outhouse. Father Meme once offered a prayer for the start of the high school basketball tournament and bloodied the court.

Father Conan Whitty was a very serious monk at Saint John's Abbey, the Benedictine Monastery in Minnesota, but he abused students and seminarians for many years and was finally sent to the Servants of the Paraclete, a congregation treatment center in Jemez Springs, New Mexico. Priests are treated there for narcotic, alcoholic, and sexual abuse problems. The crimes of sexual abuse and the actual treatment were secret, and prurient priests were protected by deceptive bishops. Father Whitty abused children everywhere, and, after a year at the Servants of the Paraclete, he was sent to parochial service at the mission church on the reservation. This cynical practice, to send lecherous priests to native missions where they sexually abused more children, was a common practice of the bishops. And, you might ask, how were we to know?

Father Meme arrived at the Indian Mission Church of the Snow with his copper bathtub, as you know, and complained about his nosebleeds. He abused Pants and Bear, the other two altar boys, and a few weeks later took me alone to the spectacular fireworks at Leech Lake. I had actually repressed the memories of that wicked priest and his miserable death in the fish house, a proper sacrifice on the ice, but then about thirty years ago he suddenly, by shock and pain of heart, came to mind at a funeral service, by every crude grope and priestly stain. I was a journalist at the time, and the city editor ordered me to investigate the tragic death by suicide of Dane White, a native boy confined in a county jail. I drove overnight to attend the funeral the next morning.

I would write about my own suicide.

Suicide was my close companion at night and on that path to the mission church. God surely would have forgiven me, an abused altar boy. I was fascinated by suicide, by the mirage of an absolute separation, the end of my hand trembling, shame and memories. Suicide could have been my paradise. Gorgeous, my great uncle, saved me, he encouraged me and the other altar boys to conspire and outmaneuver the wicked Father Meme. Pants and Bear must have thought about suicide too, but the day after we sacrificed the priest we never spoke to each other again, never. Not even on the path, not at school. No one ever mentioned the priest. I worried at the time that the priest was so wicked, maybe he was embodied only in my dreams. Maybe he was only a *wiindigoo*, the winter monster in a terrible nightmare, but how could three altar boys have the very same horrible dream? The *anishinaabe* word *giiwanaadingwaam* means to have a bad dream or a nightmare. The altar boys shared the nightmare of the *wiindigoo* priest. Pants quit school and moved to California. Bear recently retired after a career in the military. I am the only altar boy who returned to the reservation.

Sneeze died a few years later. I held him in my arms for three days, and then he tried to sneeze but lost his breath. I buried him near my father in the mission cemetery. Sneeze was not a pagan, but he barked at priests. Gorgeous carved an image of my dog on a thick plank that marked the grave. I know, *madame*, you are very considerate, the scene is truly unforgettable. Perhaps you would like to visit the cemetery? Yes, sometime later in the week. I assume you are staying in the casino hotel.

Please, listen to this despicable, tragic scene of the story. The county attorney indicted Father Conan Whitty for sexual abuse of two minors, a native teenage boy and his younger sister, while he was in treatment at the Servants of the Paraclete. Foster parents had abandoned the children. They were lonesome orphans on the road from Jemez Springs. The minors were waiting for a ride at a grocery store near the treatment center. Whitty was arrested nude with the children at a trashy roadhouse motel near Santa Fe, New Mexico.

Yes, *madame*, you are very perceptive, the priest should have been tried and convicted in tribal court, but the state had assumed jurisdiction of the case. Diocesan lawyers and treatment advocates were very persuasive in court. Whitty testified that the couple tried to steal his money and had ordered him at gunpoint to remove his clothes. The county sheriff, however, provided convincing forensic evidence of telltale semen in various orifices of the native children. Whitty was indirectly motivated by his lawyers to protect the church from shame by the practice of mental reservations, or, in other words, clerical perjury under oath. The church once sanctioned a double court system, church and civil courts. The peculiar practice of sworn testimony with mental reservations, however, is not sanctioned, at least not openly, by canon law. The priest was released from the indictment and was sent directly to our reservation. Recently, a nun refused to reveal in court what she had already written in a formal complaint: that the accused priest had sexually molested a child in the confessional. Testimony by mental reservations evokes the ancient doctrine that protected the church from scandal. Sacrifice the child, in other words, to save the Roman Catholic Church. Rightly, Father Meme was sacrificed to save the altar boys.

No, not really, *madame*, a truly terrible, terminal story would be one of absolute victimry. The altar boys refused to be priestly victims. We were never native victims, although the priest pursued us as sexual prey. Yes, we were casualties of his perversions and bear that by memory, but we sacrificed that depraved priest with coup sticks at the fish house see.

Dane White cinched a wide, black, studded belt around his neck and hanged himself, death by suicide in a solitary jail cell. He was thirteen years old. No one could understand why a gentle, native boy, barely a teenager, could be held as a criminal for more than forty days at the Wilkin County Jail in Minnesota. His only crime was truancy. Yes, you are right, truancy is not a crime. Dane ran away from school and his father to live with his native grandmother across the state border in Sisseton, South Dakota. I ran with him that afternoon, and you would too, *madame*, to be with a warmhearted grandmother. We are too late, even by this story, and now we are weakened by his suicide. Dane lost his dreams, a narrow sense of liberty. He was overcome by loneliness, cast aside by the court, and forsaken by his callous father.

I wrongly accused the sheriff of the injustice, forty days alone for truancy, but he too was deeply hurt by the suicide. The sheriff told me he could not release the boy until the case was reviewed by the juvenile court. The judge was on vacation, a big game hunter in camouflage clothes, and postponed the court hearing several times. The father had actually signed a criminal warrant against his own son to teach him a lesson, a terminal lesson about truancy. Yes, precisely, the father should have been tried for abandonment, cruelty, and the cause of suicide.

The sheriff said he took the boy with him in the patrol car on county business during the day. He and his wife took the boy home for dinner. Dane, however, was forever alone at night, locked behind the bars. He waited in silence for the judge, and then decided that suicide was his only choice. The daily kindness of the sheriff and generosity of his wife were a terrible contradiction, heartbreak, and tragic irony. Cared for by day, locked away by night. I can hardly bear to imagine his sense of desolation. Dane was lost and waited forever to run again to his grandmother. The juvenile justice system trivialized natives and brushed aside the ordinary respect for a child with a reasonable cause to live with his grandmother. Dane endured stray pity, censure as a native, faulty gestures of authority, and he waited to run across the border, any border. His suicide hurts my heart. Yes, someone must have worried about his absence.

I asked the sheriff to leave me alone for a few minutes in the jail. I slowly closed the cell door and leaned on the inside of the bars. The silence was haunting, every turn, an echo. I heard the roar of a diesel truck in the distance. I imagined his courage, at first, the tease and bravado of adult time in jail, the stories we would have told our friends, the occasional, dangerous camaraderie of other prisoners, and then, after a week or two, our separation, the heavy sense of isolation, and the cruelty of silence. Shadows moved across the bars, traces of memory. There were very few other prisoners that month, and no one was there for more than a few days. Dane must have walked in circles to the end of his life. He died by suicide just above me in that jail cell. I lost my breath for a minute.

Father Meme came to mind in that jail, he caught me alone once again, his cold hand on mine. I was hurt by traces of my past and very sensitive to suicide that afternoon, after so many years of suppressed and restrained memories. I could not endure another cold touch of that priest, not even by remembrance or exoneration of his sacrifice. I cannot easily recount the evil at the heart of that winter priest, and, in the same sense, who can account for the mysterious power that rescues the heart from the monsters of the church? These severe spiritual forces and furies are found in the same sanctuaries, counterpractices of priests at the same seminaries and missions. I bear this torment forever.

I know, *madame*, this is a terrible story that would not have been told if someone, anyone, cared enough to let that boy run to his grandmother. She loved him and had taken care of him for many years when his mother ran away. That thin, old native covered her mouth with her hand because she had no teeth. I visited her unpainted house after the funeral and felt secure there, heartened by her presence. Naturally, she covered her mouth, and the smiles raised her cheeks. She reminded me of my grandmother who was always at peace with teases and humor, and never a victim of dentistry or poverty. The pale floral linoleum patterns were cracked at the corners and worn black on the path to the tiny kitchen. Stiff, faded clothes were hung to dry over the space heater, and the house was filled with the moist scent of kerosene. I was at home, truly at peace. Dane was with me, in my heart and memory that afternoon, as his grandmother remembered the boy who was born with a great smile. She told me that the men who stole his smile would never be at peace. Dane was the one with the generous smile in every box camera picture she showed me. I was deeply moved when she related how you could always see his smile on the street, at the grocery, on a train, even in the country jail. His smile is in the world, and he is never alone.

I must describe the funeral that morning, not my published news story, but rather my intense personal responses, the punch and power of memory. The Reverend William Keohane conducted the services at Saint Catherine's Indian Mission Church in Sisseton, South Dakota. The Mission, established by the Oblates of Mary Immaculate, must have been decorated by a fussy cleric, crowded with furniture, obstructive banners and regalia, and yet familial, but there was a strong sense of absence, as if the spiritual center and sentiments were pretended, mere posture and performance rather than a grateful heart. The congregation barely voiced two hymns in the Dakota language, and you must wonder for whom the hymns were sung. Some polyglot spirit of suicide, the mighty native teases of monotheism, the more obvious rituals of dominance, or the memory of Saint Catherine of the Wheel?

Later the story of Catherine of Alexandria came to mind, a saint and martyr venerated in the name of the Fourteen Holy Helpers. The holy story is that she was tortured on the wheel, beheaded, and then rescued by angels. I could not resist an unholy analogy, Saint Dane White of the Wilkin County Jail, and if angels were smiles, he was rescued as the native saint of suicide. I was sidetracked by the service, the actual sound of the hymns was not inspired or energetic. Father Keohane, decorated in bright vestments, asked the Lord to remember Dane in his kingdom, and with that provocative, unintended irony, he turned and pointed to an enormous, awkward painting of the Last Supper mounted behind the altar of the mission church. Dane is here, chanted the priest, in the background of the banquet table. I turned on the hard bench ready to escape this incredible, uncritical service. Not a single word or worthwhile gesture, solemn or otherwise, about the duplicities of care and comfort for a child abandoned by the saints, missions, state institutions, or even the banqueters of holy repast. Surely, if the priest could project a dead native child, the last supper of a suicide, in the convenient background of a holy banquet, he could have sensed, after some forty days in jail, the lonesome presence and generous smile of Dane White.

I am truly troubled, pained, *madame*, hurt in my heart by these memories, the priestly abuse of solemn words and touch, mine and so many others in the world. I was much too vulnerable as an altar boy to appreciate the deceptions of funeral services. Most people come for the rituals, the music and stories, some for the tease of mortality and death, but never to prosecute the cultural and spiritual criminals of the church, and yet that might be the only way to expose the corruption of priests and bishops who have abandoned children to save the reputation of the papacy and Vatican City.

My funeral sermon at the mission would have indicted the church and state for child abandonment and crimes against the peace of natives. My heart was pounding with fear and rage, fear of the sudden recovery of repressed memories of an abusive priest, and rage because the service should have been held that morning in the Wilkin County Jail. Dane White was alone with the hymns and banquets of the mission. Father Keohane should have simulated the actual suicide.

Hold my vestments, he should have said to the parishioners. Then he would cinch the wide belt around his thick neck and hang himself for the service in the cell. The mission chorus, close to the bars, would sing the hymns in ironic tones, a blues funeral service. I would shout lines of poetry by Dylan Thomas: Do not go gentle into that good night. Rage, rage against the dying of the light. Dane White, rage, rage against the empire church, the chase of light, rage against the sacraments and mockery of justice.

Dane White was a native renounced by the church and court. His adolescent visions and fancies were brushed aside in forty days and forty nights behind bars, no better than a prison. He had no voice, no tease, no friends, no play, no humor, no clothes, no home, no parents, no protection, no love, no sense of presence, no ordinary nights and rights, and no one heard his stories. Dane was forever alone and could not endure the turn of a blind eye, that passive pity. Now the priest must hang from the bars, burn his neck, a stigmata for the death of this boy. The service is suicide, vindication for abuse, not a banquet of disciples.

The Catholic services concluded on a cold, cloudy autumn morning. Six school friends carried the gray metal coffin from the mission church. The strong wind raised their hair and coat lapels. Dane had one more chance to arise from the dead, to show the truth of that priestly gesture to the banquet table. He might have shared his studded black belt with the priest, but he would never return as a native only to genuflect in a prison. There were fifteen cars in the funeral procession to Saint Peter's Cemetery. The native pallbearers removed their honoring ribbons at the end of the service and placed them on the coffin. A cold wind rushed across the grassy slope and carried the ribbons to the grave.

Naniizaanizi Gakiiwe

I was convinced you would return to the Mayagi Ashandiwin Restaurant for the blue pheasant, if for no other reason. The native cuisine is memorable, almost *cuisine minceur*, and so are the stories of the menu. The council chairwoman told me that you had decided to stay on the reservation for at least a week. I am delighted, *madame*, you have found good reasons to continue your research on native progeny and states of sovereignty. The course of blood, nature, and counterpoint cultures can hardly be hurried in the hyperspace of our reservation. I am doubly pleased, actually, because we have the chance to dine together several more times. Basile Hudon, who assumed the obvious, has reserved our sunset table.

Peter Vezina has already prepared our drinks, Hendrick's Gin, as you promised to consider, with tonic water and cucumber. Please, you select the wine for dinner, French or California. You are quite right, this is already our place, and you are very sympathetic to ask about my manuscript. I am hesitant to reveal my adolescent temper, the poses of experience, or my strategic appreciation of innocence, and now even more unsure of the fear and rage of my memories at that time, and each scene, a few pages of reminiscence, uncovers contradictions and structural irony. The altar boys, in the end, were not victims, but my words, one by one, turn on that very prosecution. The priest was sacrificed, after all, and he rightly deserved to be the scapegoat. Still, you see my torment in every sentence and scene as if my stories are revealed in actual time. My stories as a journalist were more easily composed by time and situations, not by a literary stream of consciousness. The point of view or position of the narrator in autobiographical stories eluded me at first, too many salutes to instance, the tense of motion and memory, the ceremonial prompts and burdens of altar service, but then the narrative voice was clear, that mysterious moment when the tease of an interior storier creates a sense of presence, a character with a distinctive mental state who is not the author. I wrote a few pages this morning about my relatives who published the first newspaper on the reservation.

Look, the sun reaches into the wispy clouds, only the slightest orange curtain rises above the mirage of a horizon. The touch of light in the red pines is more elusive than the shimmer of the sunset yesterday. The rosy hues are muted on the waves, easy waves, your face, our hands, that tender shine at dusk. Sometimes the sunset delivers a great blaze of colors, and at other times the tones of light are drawn out of our bodies. I see that light arise in your face, your hands, my hands, in the ravens on the dock, cedar waxwings in the sumac, late summer hues of our creation. I am not always so romantic, so out of breath over sunsets, but the twilight haunts me, the last rush of light turns an unsure mood and memory. I have never been truly at ease in the dark. The priest abused the altar boys at night, late at night, and sometimes in the dark confessional by day. I am always rescued by the sunrise.

Sunsets are never the same by time or season, and yet that ordinary experience creates a sense of chance and natural reason in my stories. I once thought these common observations were profound notions, philosophical values that actually changed my perceptions of natural motion, daily events, and interpretations of experience. My inquiries as a journalist were mostly based on the customary associations of nature, and, likewise, natural reason and my appreciation of chance. I frequently asked politicians and public officials to choose a conventional, familiar metaphor from nature to compare and clarify a political strategy or legislative point. Hubert Humphrey, the former mayor, senator, and vice president, was a seasoned politician, a steady master of rural metaphors that he used to modulate the dominance, compromises, and inadvertence of federal policies. Senator Eugene McCarthy, however, was more elusive as a politician. He was a literary artist who sometimes mystified his audiences with moody poetic images. McCarthy graduated from Saint John's University in Minnesota, and he might have been influenced by some of the same teachers and monks who abused students and altar boys at reservation missions.

The Benedictine Monks at Saint John's Abbey first touched my heart by choral music, and then the priest silenced me by his greedy touch and sexual abuse. My heart was bright, light, truly at peace, and my body soared above the nave in the magical turns of light, the reds and blues of the stained church windows. I was twelve years old, a lonesome altar boy converted that late summer morning by the glorious sound of Gregorian chants. I never again experienced that moment of ethereal rhythm. That perfect sensation of deliverance comes to me now in dreams, and with some humor, a sense of eternal peace, but only after so many years. I have awakened many nights to the gruesome memory of that priest and tried to retreat to my dreams. You must appreciate the irony, *madame*, that my ecstatic, ethereal conversion is ascribed to that wicked priest. The "very life of the just is a burden to the wicked" is one of the most memorable passages from the *Life and Miracles of Saint Benedict*. The native altar boys were the just, and the priest was wicked.

Saint John's Abbey Church could have been my landmark of sacred remembrance. Father Meme ruined the virtue of that ecstasy. My memories of that time were obstructed by the shame of his sexual perversions. I returned to the abbey, a decade later, to see the new spectacular church designed by Marcel Breuer. The Bell Banner, a massive concrete monument, seemed to absolve my fear and shame of the priests and monks. Yes, *madame*, this was a dangerous passage for me. The cross in the tower was cut from white pine, and the bells had been moved from the old abbey church. My memories of abuse were distracted in the baptistery by the bronze statue of the ascetic prophet, Saint John the Baptist. I entered the great nave and remembered my transformation as an altar boy in the old church. The stained glass windows in the new church covered the entire façade, and my heartbeat turned to waves in the glory of morning light. The stained glass was abstract in the new church, magical by diffusion and lambency. The windows in the old church were scenes derived by scripture and images of Benedictine Saints. I was twice transformed by the magnificent turns of light, and the abusive monks would never enter my memories of the new church.

The Benedictine choirs, liturgical chants, and sacred music by the monks continue to inspire me, and my dreams of that moment are almost worth the priestly abuse, and only conceivable, as you know, *madame*, because we justly sacrificed the priest that winter at the fish house. There is indeed a natural reason of sacrifice.

Father Meme invited the altar boys to visit Saint John's Abbey Church about a hundred miles south of the reservation. This was the first abbey church, now named the Great Hall. I had been an altar boy for about two weeks and was very excited to travel with my friends and the priest. I remember the day so clearly. Saturday, and the three altar boys sat in the back seat of a station wagon on that bright, beautiful summer morning. My mother bought me a new pair of shoes. Sneeze and the ravens tried to warn me, but there was too much excitement to overcome. The priest drove much too fast, and almost missed a turn because his nose started to bleed. Pants handed him a towel as we approached the abbey and church. The jerky starts, stops, and turns almost made me sick. The altar boys were silent in the back seat.

Father Meme parked the car near Saint Benet Hall. Pants and Bear leaped from the back seat and ran around several buildings and into the Quadrangle of Saint John's Church. The priest was very excited and chased them in circles and then into the church with a bloody towel over his nose. I was alone and had already entered the baptistery, touched the bowl of holy water, made the sign of the cross, and entered the church. I remember a warm, moist, and gentle rush of air, as if the space was truly sacred, a creation mystery. The monks were dressed in black robes and standing by their seats in the choir stalls. I walked slowly, with hesitation, down to the nave, and then, suddenly, the church was vibrant with the sound of sacred music. I caught my breath, truly overcome by the spirited sound that touched my heart, even my arms, fingers, and eyes seemed to move spontaneously with the music. The church was alive, the light by the stained windows moved at my side. The sound of choral music was new to me as an altar boy, spacious and emotive, a great cadence in my heart. I thought about my father and sensed his presence in the church.

The monks raised their black music books and sang Gregorian chants. I moved slowly, closer to the choir, ready to be consumed forever by the sound of the plainchant voices. That moment in the church, *madame*, was truly memorable, my first ecstatic sense of creation. I once risked the thin ice in spring, and in summer the dangerous rapids and whirlpools of the river, an adolescent tease of mortal peril, but the choral music created a sense of peace rather than an adventure in the natural world. There, magical scenes of blue and red light by the stained glass windows spread across the altar and faces of the monks. *Gloria in Excelsis Deo*, Glory to God in the Highest, *Cum Sancto Spiritu in gloria Dei Patris, Amen*, With the Holy Spirit, in the glory of God the Father, Amen. Every turn and trace of sound touched me with a sense of grace. The plainchant modes and recitation of tones, the inspired cadence of the choir, and the mighty vibrancy of the pipe organ delivered me to a moment of ecstasy. The music was my conversion, my only conversion, and nothing would ever be the same.

Amen, Alleluia.

Father Meme showed us the sumptuous, carved natural wood confessionals, the sacramental chapel, and the liturgical paintings of fish and saints. Bear mocked the saints and stout fish, and we tried not to laugh in church. The priest, however, encouraged our adolescent humor, but his pose was gross, repulsive, and not funny. You might wonder, how could the curious altar boys not know that the priest wanted only our sexual favor? I could not imagine at the time the priest only wanted to touch my penis and masturbate with me in the confessional. He had no interest in my spirit. I know, *madame*, who could conceive of an ordained priest having an orgasm over an altar boy? Certainly not the altar boys. The priest marched out of the church to the entrance of the Monastic Residences. On the way he hurried to show us the cloister and library. Father Meme seemed to have many friends among the monks at the abbey. He introduced each altar boy to a monk named Roger Placid Chrisp. The Benedictine brother had a hollow back and leaned forward as he walked. He was short, thin, and very friendly. At first glance, *madame*, you might have admired him with amused curiosity. His hair was shiny, black as a raven, and shaggy at the sides. Father Meme embraced the monk, a rather tight cuddle, and the altar boys turned away. I blushed when the priest and monk actually kissed each other, on the cheeks, neck, and mouth. We heard the priest use a devoted name, Petit Swayback. The monk invited us into his monastic residence, and, without warning, asked each of the altar boys about masturbation and sexual fantasies. Strange, indeed, *madame*, and we were nervous, of course, and avoided the question with clumsy laughter, because we had no idea what the word meant. Pants thought the word was in Latin. Bear said the word was sacred. The monk was very charming and told us that he became a teaser because as a child he was always teased as a swayback. The altar boys were not aware of that word either at the time. He tightened his robe to show us the inward curvature of his back. The *Manabosho Curiosa*, an arcane monastic manuscript of stories about human sex with animals, noted the word *lordosis* to describe the same curvature of the spine, the erotic posture of female animals during mating. The priest was apparently inspired by the lordosis of the monk. Brother Chrisp talked openly about his secret life as a Benedictine monk. Bear turned away when the monk tried to touch his face. Pants wrinkled his nose at the monk, a sign of distrust. I know native teasers, my relatives are teasers, and the monk was no teaser. I told the monk about the music, the voices of the choir, and my emotive responses. He was prompted by my story, for some reason, to reach out and touch my shoulders, back, and chest with his hands, probably the only natural touch of the day, although touching my chest and back seemed to be unusual at the time. Father Meme suggested that we walk to the nearby student beach on Lake Sagatagan. Brother Chrisp walked close to me down the narrow path to the beach located behind the Monastic Residences. He commented on my new shoes. I was cautious, as you can imagine, and continued talking about how the music had touched my heart. I could only assume that as a monk he too was inspired by the same plainchant music of the Gregorian chants. I told the monk that the name of the lake sounded like *zagataagan*, the native *anishinaabe* word for tinder, or punk used to start a fire. He suddenly stopped on the path and hugged me much too tightly. I thought at the time that his embrace was rather intense for my comment on the native name of the lake. His body exuded the same scent as the priest, cedar and winter rose. I pushed him away and ran toward the beach house by the lake. Pants and Bear were already in a canoe paddling with the priest to the nearby chapel. Brother Chrisp reached for my hand, an awkward gesture, and then motioned for me to follow him along the path to the Stella Maris Chapel, Star of the Sea, on Lake Sagatagan. Pants and Bear were standing outside the chapel when we arrived by foot. My sense of the Catholic world changed forever at that moment. The priest was nude, he stood alone at the altar inside the chapel. Pants said he had removed his clothes in the canoe. I could hardly believe that his fleshy body was almost cloudy, pale coral by color, and an apparent rosy rash spread from the thick red hair on his crotch to his chest. He shouted at me to join hands at the chapel. I balked and tried to turn away. The priest masturbated near the altar rail. Swayback held me tightly from behind, his hands low on my thighs, and forced me to watch the priest masturbate. Brother Chrisp pressed his hard penis against my back. Pants and Bear were scared and ran back to the beach house. I followed, and together we hurried in silence to the Quadrangle. For some reason we felt secure in the church gardens. The altar boys did not speak on the ride back to the reservation. Later our fear and willies were overcome when we mocked the nickname used by the priest. Brother Chrisp became the creepy Swayback. I never told my mother about the nude priest or the monk with a boner on my back. Shelter would never believe me, but always praised my imagination. Gorgeous and Sneeze never doubted my stories. Sunday morning at early Mass we carried out our duties as if nothing had happened the day before at the monastery. I lighted the altar candles, sounded the sacred bells, and waited with the other altar boys at the side of the priest. He leaned over the altar stone and, all of a sudden, blood ran down his chin, stained his vestments and the altar. Pants handed the priest a white towel, an ordinary practice at the mission. The ravens warned me once again, croaked loudly down the stone chimney. I cleaned the stone of his blood and threw the towels into the outhouse. Then, later, there was blood and semen on the bench in the confessional. Father Meme ordered the altar boys to return to the mission that afternoon. Naturally we were anxious that he would either abuse or release us from our altar duties. Not really, you see, he was even more determined to seduce than to reveal or excuse the altar boys. He actually calculated his abuse by a bold invitation to hear stories that late afternoon from a copy of a frayed manuscript, the *Manabosho Curiosa*. Our wicked priest lived by manners contrary to natural reason, and he teased with erotic stories of human sex with animals. He was obsessed with smutty sex, and we soon learned to humor his perversions.

There, you see, *ma chère amie*, you have only encouraged my stories into the twilight. We must now consider the menu and wine over priests and missions. Yes, a natural choice, *miinan mayagi bine*, the blue pheasant. For me, *giigoonhwaaboo*, the fish soup tonight. Pierre told me he has fresh *ogaa*, walleye, caught only two hours ago. You are obviously more confident about French *cuvée* white wines, but the Landmark Overlook Chardonnay would be an excellent wine with our entrées.

You are quite right, *madame*, natural reason is not an easy concept for some people, and that, as you know, is a truism because monotheistic canons of nature deny chance as a source of reason.

Gorgeous, my great uncle, was a teaser by nature. He would never practice the sentiments of chance because it would not have been natural to practice chance, and he never practiced reason either. Chance was wonder and surprise, not a practice. Gorgeous created figures and tropes from nature to secure his word shows, the context, conversations, and descriptive means. Somehow his stories inspired visual memories of scenes, not mere words or the recitation of liturgy.

You are right to ask, *madame*, for at least one instance of natural reason by description or story. No one has ever asked me to prove the point, and that is because natural reason is a state of consciousness, not a core, crux, or keynote. Surely you would agree that spiders create intricate, concise, perfectly woven webs by memory, an ordinary observation and appreciation of the natural world. Do you know anyone who can create silky, circular spider webs overnight? Not me, but the creative act of a spider is natural reason. Gorgeous might say that federal agents are lonesome spiders at the outhouse door, or, wise spiders wait in the shadows, needy lovers break the webs. Sneeze, my dog, had more memory by nose than a priest by his rituals, and that is ordinary natural reason. So, send that nasty priest a bucket of blueberries, an elusive image that meat cooked with blueberries is much more tender, and a natural color at the same time. Cook the priest blue and tender, the two contingencies that might improve his coral body and surly character. Now, consider this serious but ironic instance of natural reason, a noisy raven seems to warn a human that a cougar or a bear is close at hand, but, more likely, the raven cued the bear that human prey is nearby. Ravens warn the cougar and bear to share the prey. Many monotheists would rather be devoured as tragic prey than accept chance and natural reason at the heart of their stories.

Your toast, *à votre santé*, is very generous, and may you always raise the steady heartbeat of visual stories over the dominance of cold monotheistic liturgy. I hear the steady, lively beat of your heart, *ma chère madame*, over the priestly count of sacraments.

Father Meme was the fourth priest at the Indian Mission of the Snow. I know, the name is obvious, ridiculous, but the priest who founded the mission arrived by chance in the fiercest snowstorm of the century. Three feet of snow overnight and mighty drifts buried the *wiigiwaaman*, or the wigwams on the reservation. Gorgeous told me only the chimneys of log cabins rose above the snow, a sign of modernity. Father Fusco was from Palermo, Sicily. He was the first of four priests who vanished, one each generation, in the winter on the reservation. Fathers Fusco, Nikolaus, De Lorin, and our Meme have gone missing and never returned. Really, no one seems to care what happened to the four priests. Yes, *madame*, you wonder, why would any priest accept a parochial mission on the reservation? God's will, tender mercies, dissipations, to be sure, and the rest is chance. The ravens have taunted the priests and marched around the snow mission for more than a century. My ravens warned me that the priest was about his wicked moves of mercy. They soared over the mission several times a day, walked with care through the grave markers, and preened, huge shiny wings, perched on the stone chimney in time for Mass on Sunday. Truly, the ravens croaked at every service, and the ravens were more than a flutter of blackbirds in the face of Saint Benedict. Father Meme, and no doubt the previous three priests, cursed the guttural croaks of the ravens, the black devils of the reservation. My ravens were always protectors, and the perfect agents provocateurs of natural reason.

The sunsets create a state of mind, a distinctive mood, spirit, traces and tributes of chance, and for me, a sense of uncertain associations. The magical hues reach into my uneasy horizon of memory. Do you sometimes want to hold back the night? Hold back the memory of lonesome nights? Not forever, of course, but long enough to heal the fear of separation and then return to the early creases of light. The birds vanish every night, and rightly so, but where do they go? Bats reverse the turn of light, and rush out at the precise instance of twilight. Consider the natural reason of ravens and bats, some of us are happier by day, and others wait for the cover of night. I wonder, *ma chère madame*, would you be a twilight bat or a wise raven? Naturally, the wise raven of *liberté* at the Indian Mission Church of the Snow.

The ravens always captured my attention and imagination, even as a child. I truly admire their concentration, humor, and tricky play. Ravens could easily reign on the reservation. Maybe they have, always in the visual sway of native memory. Sneeze treated them with great respect, but he maintained an escape distance. There, you can see the faint shadows of red pine reach across the decoys on the dock and break on the waves. Shadows so faint they evaporate in the slightest breeze. The ravens turn, hesitate, and stumble in the shadows on the shoreline. Why does a raven roll over on his back and play dead? The other ravens bounced in circles and appear to mock the performance. Maybe the sunset moves are a diversion, the other ravens are too close to a hidden food cache. Would you play dead to protect your food stash? Who would not protect a scanty cache and sidetrack a hungry stranger? Yet you, *madame*, did not divert my intrusion last night at the sunset table. Yes, of course, we shared the cost of our dinner. Look, the ravens are on the dock, a twilight dance, always on stage and ready to play. Where do the ravens sleep at night?

Gorgeous told me you always learn more from ravens than priests. I was five years old at the time of his advice, and the ravens were already my agents provocateurs of natural reason. Later, the ravens walked and talked with me, warned me to beware of the malicious priests and the many priestly ghosts on the twilight path to the mission. These natural encounters would have been more elusive, by chance and practice, in the city. I wonder if there are readers who would appreciate an autobiographical narrative from the point of view of a raven? No wonder native storiers named the ravens tricksters by chance and natural reason. Only a raven trickster would roll over and play dead to distract his best friends.

Father Meme was born in the wrong century, an ominous delivery much too late to live by chance and natural reason. He might have found some solace among the animals at the headwaters of the *gichiziibi*, the big river, in the fifteenth century. Probably not the fur trade, *madame*, because the menace of his cold touch would have stiffened the hides. On the other hand, certain monarchs and consorts would surely value the exotic furs of priestly perversions. Father Meme might have flourished by beastly debauchery in the fifteenth century. Native boys, at the time, were with their fathers and fur traders in canoes, not yet ready to await the vainglory of priests at the altars. The early priests turned to animals but only as sexual prey. There were no altar boys, only wild animals to abuse at the enigmatic headwaters.

The Holy Rule of Saint Benedict was declared once more by wayward monks, and a monastery was established five centuries ago at the *gichiziibi* headwaters of the Mississippi River. The monks wasted no time in the serious revisions of the immutable seventy-three rules, such as obedience, authority of the abbot, practices of prayer, weighty faults, food, drink, clothes, oratory, labor, and how boys are to be corrected by measures that provide for severe fasts and harsh beatings as disciplinary cures. There were only native boys around the headwaters, and they were warned by ravens, bears, and relatives to stay away from the monks. These new, inspired monastic rules included sensual pleasures with specific animals, those animals found eager to participate with the monks at the headwaters. The monks were stimulated, maybe tricked and goaded, to pursue natural reason and wild animals for sexual amusement and diversions. A native historian told me that the monks were secure in their new sensual practices because sex with an animal was not a violation of the vows of celibacy. I repudiated the convictions of monotheists that animals were created as mere targets or clients of dominion, and without souls, or even the inadvertent godly grace of salvation. Would you support these wayward monks in their beastly sexual practices? Clearly, there was not much chance of marriage or progeny. I wonder, though, if most of the monks considered sex with a wild animal more of a sensual covenant than mere carnal prostitution?

I must ask, *madame*, for your permission to continue with these stories of the lusty monks at the headwaters. My point, although obscure, is that the priest at the mission might not have abused the altar boys if he had only practiced the pleasures of sex with wild animals. I bear some animus, as you know, for monastic sex with animals, but the monks and priests were more prey than hunter, and they were constrained to lure and assure an animal by more than promises of coition. Surely the ravens would circle and croak over every instance of arousal and ejaculation. Would you agree, that this new woodland monastery at the source of the great river was the actual demise of monotheism?

The *Manabosho Curiosa*, an atavistic manuscript about the sensual beastly pleasures of monastic monks at the headwaters, was discovered by the distinguished antiquarian book collector Pellegrine Treves. The illustrated manuscript was first sold at an auction in London. I was a journalist at the time and wrote a feature story about this manuscript, but the city editor would not permit descriptive sexual scenes with animals to be published in a family newspaper. Rightly so, but obviously my story promoted the circulation of the *Manabosho Curiosa* in translation. Treves was an honorable collector, and he refused to accept the circumspection of historians that the manuscript was inauthentic or blasphemous; however, others were even more cautious because there was no decisive evidence that monks were ever at the headwaters of the *gichiziibi*, the great river. The *anishinaabe* know otherwise.

The word *manabosho* in the title of the curiosa is a variation of the word *naanabozho*, the name of the protean native trickster of *anishinaabe* oral stories. The word *curiosa*, erotic curiosities, or *pornographie*, as you know, describes the incomparable erotic trickster stories in this manuscript. Treves was convinced that the *Manabosho Curiosa* was authentic, although he refused to take a position on pleasures of human sex with animals. Scientific studies of the parchment and the stylistic patterns of the calligraphy suggest that the manuscript could have been created in the fifteenth century, or even earlier. The parchment was made with the skins of animals common to the headwaters at the time, and an analysis of the chemical composition of the paint used to create the calligraphic script and pictures contributed to the evidence that the curiosa was authentic. Whisper, the healer, might have transcribed the stories of monks in the curiosa, but credence and praise remains with the Benedictine monks at Monte Cassino. Most readers, as you can imagine, were more interested in the actual stories than in the authenticity. French authors wrote bawdy stories about the same time.

The Black Death had driven the Benedictine monks to sea with their venerable monastic rules and manuscripts. The monks sailed, apparently, on the Great Lakes, portaged inland a century before the fur traders, and landed at the headwaters in the late summer at least two decades before the adventures of Christopher Columbus. The Holy Rule of Saint Benedict at *gichiziibi* has become the source of trickster stories of natural reason and erotic irony. The monastic silence of monasteries was converted by the third winter to the rules of *naanabozho*, the trickster creator of the natural tease of seasons and stories. Fleury, the first monastery at the headwaters, was a *wiigiwaam*, a native wigwam or arched structure constructed by *anishinaabe* women. Rightly, the monks must have been worried about *gaaskanazo*, or Whisper, the nickname of the old woman who carried a beaver stick and was circled by four ravens. I heard stories about the old woman, a healer, from my grandmother, and she carried a sumac or lilac stick as protection. The altar boys used common lilac and birch beaver sticks to beat the priest in the fish house. The lilac wood is strong, resilient, and a curved stick is a potent weapon.

The monks endured two mild winters, but only by the trust of natives. Whisper and her ravens lived alone near the headwaters. She teased the monks at every turn and eventually enticed them to participate in the *debwe*, the native heart dance late in the third, severe winter. The *anishinaabe* word *debwe* means to be truthful, or to literally tell the truth. The heart dance was a marvelous practice to survive the severe woodland winters, but, in this instance, the dance mocked the severe pious services of the monastic monks. Whisper was a formidable healer, and she easily seduced the monks with erotic animal moves and stories. The snow was heavy, crusted, and some of the monks could not endure the silence, the monastic desolation, and solitary rituals in the harsh, cold winter far from home. Some of the monks were ecstatic, liberated by the erotic dances, but the pleasure caused a separation, an absolute schism in the monastery. Fleury, the first monastery, continued the decorous, severe monastic rules at the *gichiziibi* headwaters by godly grace. Monte Cassino, the second, breakaway monastery, declared and founded the new rituals and rules of the *debwe* heart dancers on the eastern shore of Bad Medicine Lake. The Monte Cassino monks created an erotic New World practice of the Holy Rule of Saint Benedict.

The *Manabosho Curiosa* contains the actual pictures and stories of the sexual conversions of Benedictine monks with the animals at the *debwe* heart dance. The early entries in the manuscript describe prurient scenes of common monastic masturbation. The entries on masturbation, however, ended with the stories of the seasonal heart dances. I must continue, *madame*, in this rather indiscreet manner for a few more minutes. The later manuscripts revealed that several monks were aroused by a precious snowshoe hare and masturbated on her soft winter coat. The natural reach of the snowshoe, poised on her long rear legs, was so erotic that some monks could not hold back and ejaculated prematurely. The Monte Cassino abbot declared in several stories that the monks and bears were natural masturbators. Whisper convinced the monks that the bears taught men how to masturbate, but not in Latin. The bears were human then, and masturbation was the primordial signature of natural reason, chance, and trickery. The monks told erotic stories about the sleek river otter. The stories revealed the beastly eroticism of the monks, how they were aroused by the webbed toes and sensuous moves of the river otter at the heart dances.

Pellegrine Treves, the antiquarian book collector, circulated several copies of the translated manuscript of the *debwe* heart dances to selected authors and scholars around the world. He was eager to share the stories, but the conditions of circulation were explicit that the manuscript was not to be published without permission. Treves, however, allowed the usual fair and reasonable editorial use of the manuscript. He was concerned about manners, clerical censure, and the commercial protection of the curiosa. The manuscript would be circulated with discretion, care, and great sensitivity, but there were many extreme distractions, abusive revisions, and altered editions sold as clerical pornography.

Father Meme arrived at the mission with a revised copy of the *Manabosho Curiosa*. The manuscript, frayed and stained, was packed with photographs and other books in a grocery bag. The priest told some of the animal sex stories to arouse the altar boys. Pants found the manuscript later in a bureau drawer, not with other books. We secretly read the stories and copied some of the scenes to share with our friends at school. The priest was always vigilant, but rather than the ordinary altar boy castigation he smiled and encouraged us to confess our sexual fantasies. He ordered us to read the heart dance stories, and, at the time, we were aware but not fully convinced of his sexual intentions or perversions until he introduced us to Brother Roger Chrisp at Saint John's Abbey. He was constantly aroused by the thought that his altar boys had read to each other the erotic stories. Once he asked me to describe the scene of the monk who was enticed by a white tailed deer at the heart dance.

Father Meme mounted the signature crucifix over his bed, as if the cross would sanction his perversions. There were three framed pictures on the chest of drawers, two of young men, and the third of Pope Pius XII with Father Marcial Maciel and more than fifty young men and boys, Legionaries of Christ. Marcial Maciel was the handsome, moody boy in the first picture, and the second picture in a red frame was Brother Roger Placid Chrisp. Only later the altar boys learned about the Legionaries of Christ.

Father Meme delivered several boxes of canned food, beans, peanut butter, and hard blocks of cheese to my mother, a rather cynical gesture to convince her that the mission was concerned about the altar boys. My mother needed the food and could hardly fault the commodity bounty, but the priest was connected to corrupt federal agents who provided commodities, or *ashandiwin*, to reservations. The gifts of food by the priest were always political strategies. The altar boys waited to learn what requital was necessary to accommodate the *ashandiwin* bounty. I mean, *madame*, he might have disregarded my mother altogether. Shelter was very poor, and she actually depended on my weekly income, mere dimes for my service as an altar boy.

Yes, *ma chère madame*, you are very perceptive, the word *ashandiwin*, commodity food or rations, is indeed the name of the restaurant, Mayagi Ashandiwin Restaurant, and the word *mayagi*, as you know, means exotic or foreign, so the name of the restaurant is ironic: Exotic Commodity Rations. I was certain you would appreciate the native irony. Truly, and you notice the second ironic name, the Good Cheer Casino.

Shelter accepted an invitation from the priest for me, in my name but not with my consent, to travel with him and the other altar boys to Lake Namakan near the border with Canada. Thirty some years ago the area was named the Voyageurs National Park. Father Meme was always crafty, deceitful, and he knew my mother would agree, and that his favor and apparent generosity would counter any of my stories about his nudity and perversions. I was sure my mother would never appreciate the corruption of the priest, and she never revealed anything untoward about the mission. Shelter gently reminded me that our ancestors were buried in the mission cemetery. Gorgeous was my only confidant, as always, and he held me to the futurity of chance and natural reason, in other words, a native way to counteract the seductions of tragic victimry. You would not believe, *madame*, how cunning that priest could be in his pursuit of fantasy sex with altar boys. Father Meme not only bribed my mother, but he even tried to persuade my great uncle, the government school, and the federal agents on the reservation to sponsor an expedition with the altar boys to the Boundary Waters Canoe Area Wilderness. The canoe lakes are part of the Superior National Forest in Minnesota. The priest boldly proposed that the altar boys would paddle under his supervision in two canoes from Gunflint Lake to Magnetic Lake, and then navigate the Granite River along the international border to Granite Lake. The priest was very persuasive and explained that the altar boys would learn about the old fur trade and portages, but he had no experience or sense of the time and distance of the area. Father Meme even declared that the portage was a memory in our blood because some of our ancestors were fur traders. Gorgeous told the federal agents that the priest was *giiwanaadizi*, truly crazy. Actually, the priest was treacherous and *naniizaanizi*, a word that means dangerous. Shelter consented, but no one else on the reservation would endorse the fantastic, priestly expedition of altar boys in the Boundary Waters. Gorgeous learned later that the deluded priest had secretly invited the Swayback, Brother Roger Chrisp. The compromise excursion and portage was by a huge rented houseboat on Lake Namakan.

Shelter was concerned that the priest would be disheartened by the denial of his portage proposal, and yet she was very pleased about the compromise. The altar boys, you see, would need no camping equipment, as the houseboat was fully furnished with cots, blankets, dishes, cooler, and stove. Pants and Bear had been on a long canoe portage with their fathers and older brothers, on the *gichiziibi* lakes of the Mississippi River. My time in a canoe was limited to nearby lakes during the wild rice seasons. I made a new slingshot from a perfect crotch of summer lilac, red tire rubber, and the tongue of an old shoe. Lilac is thin, strong, and the perfect curves make the very best slingshots. Have you ever used a slingshot? Well, then, you shall not be denied the experience.

Perhaps later in the week we can cut a crotch from local lilac, the rest is much easier to make today.

Sneeze ran close to my side for several days. He was aware that something was about to happen, and naturally he wanted to be with me. The only time my dog was left behind was the day the priest took us to Saint John's Abbey. I obviously did not want to leave him alone, but the priest would never accept my dog. Sneeze always barked at him, even at the mission, and chased the priest on the path near our cabin. Actually, my mother intervened and persuaded the priest to allow me to take my dog along on the houseboat. I understand now that the priest was desperate to be trusted by my mother, to counter any of my stories about sexual abuse. I never told her about the abuse because she would never believe me.

Now that, *madame*, is perfect, a consummate *mayagi bine*, the most magnificent pheasant breast on the reservation. Pierre clearly favors you, and he may join us soon to confirm your pleasure with words such as tender, delicate, sumptuous, and ritzy. He appreciates the word *magnifique* in response to his culinary sovereignty. The blue pheasant actually exceeds the metaphors by flavor. The most tasty, savory meals have no adequate descriptions, and so the use of *anishinaabe* words for the entrées on the menu. Yes, and the use of the native words *mayagi ashandiwin* is both exotic and ironic. You must share some of my fish soup, the walleye has a unique, natural flavor of the woodland lakes. I swear, *madame*, there are traces of ancient stone, cedar bark, and even the delicate taste of fragrant water lily. You see, even my descriptions of fresh walleye are inadequate. Yes, you are very observant, and some of my friends tease me in the same way about my choice of language and precise diction. I would rather be an exotic menu by my words than a mundane storier.

Brother Swayback Chrisp arrived by bus in Walker, Minnesota, on Monday, July 27, 1953. The altar boys waited near the hotel that morning. Three ravens bounced to the end of the dock, ready for another ungainly chase by Pants and Bear. There, you can see the actual place, although the dock has been extended since then, more than fifty years ago. I remember the precise date because my mother told me that morning about the end of the Korean War. She surveys time and dates by war, conscription, declarations of peace, and especially by the service of native soldiers. Shelter wrote to native soldiers years before the death of my father. She worried most about the war when Nazi Germany invaded France on June 5, 1940. How old were you, *madame*, at the time? Yes, of course, only a child, and your parents were wise to move to the country, Rochenbrune. I only recently read about the Nazi massacre at Oradour-sur-Glane. My mother would hear or read a story about a native soldier and write to honor his service. I was born, as you know, on the day the first peace-time conscription was enacted, October 16, 1940, a month after Congress passed the Selective Training and Service Act. My father was rejected by the military for medical reasons, weak lungs and heart, but most of his relatives and native friends on the reservation were eager to be drafted for service. Crier and my mother left the reservation partly to avoid the shame that he could not serve his country. Shelter returned to the reservation after the death of my father. Every night she wrote letters by the kerosene lamp, and she received many, many letters from natives in the military, so many letters that the post office gave her a second nickname,

Vargas Girl. My apologies, *madame*, for the obscure reference, Alberto Vargas created shapely, wholesome girls for calendars and nose art on fighter planes. French soldiers must share similar pleasures of pinup art. Yes, voluptuous and highly romanticized women of the poster wars. Shelter blushed over the nickname when she picked up the mail, but she told me stories about only three special native soldiers: Clarence Marcellais, an *anishinaabe* who was wounded twice in the first year of the Korean War; Ben Nighthorse Campbell, Northern Cheyenne, who served in the Air Force in Korea; and Mitchell Red Cloud, who was awarded the Medal of Honor posthumously by General Omar Bradley, Chairman of the Joint Chiefs of Staff. My mother had two pinups in her bedroom: Crier, my father; and Mitchell Red Cloud. The Ho Chunk warrior from Wisconsin served in the Marine Corps Raiders during the Second World War. Later he enlisted in the army and was stationed in occupied Japan before combat service in the first year of the Korean War. My mother continued to write to Corporal Red Cloud for many, many years after his death. She was convinced that his native spirit read her letters and that one day they would be together. So, you see how significant some dates are in my memory.

Father Meme and Swayback waited for the altar boys in the station wagon. They were dressed in civilian clothes and smiled as we climbed into the back seat, as if they shared a secret. The altar boys were not aware of their precise perversions, but we would soon expose their covert carnal mission on the houseboat. They were neither father nor brother to anyone. Sneeze was very excited and thrust his nose out the window. The ravens circled the station wagon for many miles that morning on the way to

Lake Namakan. The priest stopped in Bemidji, and the altar boys ran around the enormous statues of Paul Bunyan and Babe the Blue Ox. Swayback treated us to ice cream, and one scoop in a bowl for Sneeze. That was a perfect start, and the end was even better, but we had no sense of what would happen three days later on the houseboat. Bemidji was a side tour to entice the altar boys, and we were pleased by the ice cream. Swayback drove from Bemidji through Tenstrike, Blackduck, Big Falls, Little Fork, and then across to Ray and the Ash River Trail. Pants and Bear were asleep after our stop at a market in Little Fork, and that was possible only because the priest was not driving. Swayback drove just under the speed limit and was very steady. Sneeze nosed me at every scent and scene, always alert to nature. The wind was warm, clean, and carried traces of wild rose and musty cattails. The meadowlarks and redwing blackbirds sang along as we passed their posts, a lovely chorus on the road to Lake Namakan. Yes, *madame*, here is a bold, napkin road map of the journey. The highway narrowed here on the Ash River Trail. The priest was asleep, snoring as we arrived at the first docks on the river. I clearly remember my excitement at the time, the sense of freedom and adventure. There were people about in boats and the muffled sound of outboard motors on the river. There was even a restaurant. Swayback awakened the priest and announced that we would have a late lunch and then locate the rental agent for the houseboat. I ordered my favorite, a bacon, lettuce, and tomato sandwich. Pierre teased me on the lunch menu last year with a bacon sandwich in my name, *giikanaamozigan bakwezhigan*, or bacon on bread cooked over an open fire. The tease is truly deserved, almost worthy of a nickname, because my choice of food on the road was always bacon and tomato. The sandwich at the Ash River Restaurant was memorable. I could have easily eaten a second sandwich but hesitated to distract the apparent care and generosity of the brother and priest. Surprisingly the priest posed as the indulgent father, and he introduced his three altar boys to the waitress, the cook, and anyone who looked our way. We were rather shied by the turn of priestly manners. The priest even took the time to introduce my dog. Sneeze smiled and sneezed, of course, and everyone thought his name was perfect. The priest was at ease, a mood that was new to the altar boys, and we only later realized that he did not have a nosebleed until, on the third day, we stole the houseboat.

The Queen Marva houseboat seemed enormous to me at the time, about thirty feet long with three bunks for the altar boys and a double bed for the working clergy. I could not resist, *madame*, that moment of prurient irony. Sneeze was eager to board but unsure of the steady sway of the houseboat. I was hesitant too because the motion was too far from the water. We were secure in a canoe but cautious on the upper deck of a houseboat. Bear moved with the motion, imitated an old man, and then rushed to the helm and declared his discovery, the Ash River Trail. Pants unpacked the groceries in the galley. I was excited by our adventure, pirates of an unknown sea, but the priest, as always, worried me to shame. I had only been an altar boy for a few weeks, and in that time the greedy hand of the priest touched me at the fireworks, he masturbated at the chapel, and he then told sex stories about humans and animals. I must have thought that sailors and pirates faced the same perils and feats at sea. That wicked priest was my captain. Sneeze ran to the bow and barked at the people on shore. Father Meme was silent as he boarded, his ice blue eyes twitched from side to side. Swayback had negotiated the rental, paid for the fuel, noted the rules of navigation, and then started the engine. The agent pushed the houseboat away from the dock as the transmission clunked into reverse. Blue smoke spread out on the river. The steel decks shivered under the power of the engine, a constant vibration that moved though my body. Swayback was at the helm and turned the boat into the main channel of the Ash River Bay. Sneeze barked again, and the agent waved from the dock as we set sail for the new world of Lake Namakan.

The Queen Marva moved slowly on the river, the prow cutting a slight crease in the water. I remember a snake or some river beast that moved in the reeds and rousted the noisy redwing blackbirds. Two dragonflies bounced in the bright slant of sunlight, and the shoreline moved slowly past as traces of ancient memory. I wonder, *madame*, if you have ever practiced that perception of motion on a river that overtakes the instance of a secure, moored visual memory. That sense of perfect motion is by tease of seasons and turns of memory. Yes, *madame*, we must canoe on the river later in the week. We might see muskrat, river otter, and the precision plunge of a cocky kingfisher. I could have been an otter on the river, or a secretive cedar waxwing. The boat shivered, but my heart was in flight, my body as shiny as a raven or river otter. Sneeze was at my side on the bow. His nose traced the scent of every natural motion on the shoreline. We were voyageurs on an ancient river of our ancestors. I was certain, *ma chère madame*, that the altar boys were invincible warriors and voyageurs. At the same time the houseboat became our stage of a mystery play. The curious scenes were staged by three altar boys, not by saints, priest, or the swayback monk. The Ash River widened into Sullivan Bay, and the shoreline unfurled in a natural motion. The traces of ancient boulders were never a precise closure, not even in poetry. The prow pushed into the thick water, over the stone shadows of the narrow channel into the shimmer of waves on Lake Namakan.

Swayback increased the power once the houseboat cleared the channel, and turned east toward the islands and the international border. Father Meme handed us soft drinks, Doctor Pepper, and prepared two martinis, one for Swayback. The priest took over the helm and steered the houseboat toward the border. The engine roared, and the decks shuddered into the waves. The raucous gulls circled over the boat, an eye turned to any gesture of human fare, downriver to the lake, and then turned back with another boat. Scavengers are always on duty, but the gulls pose as hearty tourists, not the furtive bounce and menace of vultures, or the savage grovel of hyenas. So, would you concur, *madame*, that only humans have lost their instinct as survival scavengers? Yes, if humans could only fly. Sometimes we can imagine natural flight, once or twice, by ecstasy and in dreams, but mostly we tease that reserve and separation by the mere pitch of bread crumbs to pigeons in the park. I am a magical flier on the voices of Gregorian chants. Yes, we were on the houseboat, and the gulls turned back to the river. The priest shouted that we would dock for dinner at Cemetery Island. Swayback pointed to the tiny island on the map. Bear was worried about the name of the island and pleaded with the priest and monk that we could not eat over the graves of our native ancestors. Father Meme ignored the worries of the altar boys and slowly circled the island in search of a sandy bay to moor the houseboat. The priest had no sensitivity or respect for native traditions and clearly dishonored our ancestors. Why not, indeed, he had no respect for the altar boys. Luckily, the wind and waves increased, and the priest could not find a secure landing on the glacial island. I was convinced at the time that the native spirits of our ancestors mounted the wind to warn that wicked priest and protect the altar boys. Swayback took the helm and turned the boat slightly to the south across Blind Indian Narrows near Williams Island. The boat swayed and shivered on the choppy narrows of the lake. The priest leaned over the map, and we worried that his nose would soon start to bleed. Pants had a towel at hand, the altar boy in service to the sacred nosebleeds. Suddenly his face flushed, his hair seemed to vibrate, and he shouted that it was too late to find a harbor. The sun was low, but there was enough time to circle another island before dark. The altar boy pirates had only been to sea for a few hours, and the captain had lost his bearings. I think you are right, *madame*, the priest was more concerned about sex with the monk and the altar boys than a haven for our first dinner at sea. The priest moved to the helm and embraced the monk, his hand on the swayback. Actually, we felt more secure around the priest when he was in the arms of his lover. The irony ended when the monk turned his prurient attention to the altar boys. Father Meme was a sleazy abuser of Catholic rage and vengeance. The houseboat almost ran ashore on a tiny island while the priest and monk cuddled at the helm. Sneeze barked, we shouted, and the monk slowed the boat and turned toward the only dock on Hoist Bay. The lake was much calmer in the bay, and steadily the houseboat moved closer to the dock. Swayback had never docked a boat, but his sense of motion and distance to the narrow wooden dock was masterly. The owner rushed down from his cabin, no doubt worried that his dock was about to be crushed by a houseboat. Grateful, the man tied the boat to the dock and praised the captain. Sneeze and the altar boys waited in a solemn queue on the bow. The priest smiled and introduced the captain and cabin boys. Patrick the dock man turned cautious, not certain about how we were related, until the priest announced that we were actually altar boys and a monk. We remained silent, hoping that in our unsure and unstated way the dock man would sense the perversions of the priest and monk, and we would be saved or discovered. The priest overstated the wind and waves near Cemetery Island and Blind Indian Narrows. He told the dock man his only concern was to find a safe moorage for the night. Patrick, the dock man, and his short, stout wife, Marion, were Catholic. The religious connection ended any chance that we would be saved by strangers on a dock. Pants was hungry and asked the priest about dinner. Bear was shied by the waves in the narrows and steady sway of the boat. He walked alone into the woods to lose the sway. Sneeze ran ashore with me and never barked at the dock man. I returned to my fantasy of piracy.

The Catholics were united by their faith and tricky fate on that narrow dock, and the priest even blessed the couple as pure pilgrims at the outpost of civilization. Naturally, we were invited to stay for dinner by the pilgrims of Lake Namakan. Patrick and Marion were truly generous people, retired schoolteachers, who decided to move to a remote lakeshore cabin near the international border when their only daughter died in an automobile accident. Sneeze charmed them in an instant by his smile, as you can imagine, *madame*, and he was allowed to sit next to me at dinner. The table was set on the screen porch with a view of Hoist Bay. Patrick told the altar boys to wash their hands at the outside pump, and he never once asked about our native culture or the name of our reservation. I clearly remember my temptation at the pump, my hands under the cold water, to reveal the perversions of the priest and monk. Patrick was an honorable man, he smiled and gently teased us some about the weather and waves on the lake. Later we learned that his daughter was native, she had been adopted at an orphanage established by the Benedictines. Yes, *madame*, you are quite right, it was rather natural for me to imagine my life as an orphan in their family. I could not, of course, betray the generosity of the pilgrims by stories about a wicked priest and a prurient monk. I thought many times about my hesitation at that moment. I might have revealed the perversions at dinner, and the experiences of the altar boys would not have been the same, the priest would probably not have been sacrificed at the fish house, but when would have been the best time? At the blessing of the meal by the priest? Or, how about between servings of walleye and mashed potatoes? I might have waited to finish the meal and, as dessert was served, cleared my throat and boldly described the sexual practices, abuse, and corruption of the priest. I could have told the story of cleaning the priest's blood and semen from the confessional last Sunday. Or, why not ask the priest to talk about his naked rave and masturbation at the chapel altar rail? No, obviously, that would not have been a polite way to end a friendly dinner. There is no easy way, *madame*, for altar boys to reveal the shame of their abuse by the priest. Patrick must have been suspicious, and he should have invited me to talk about the priest. That would have been a perfect moment to end the priestly abuse, when we were alone at the outside water pump. So, the story of the wicked priest ends by sacrifice.

The loons called to each other on the bay. That haunting sound was as true and ecstatic as a plainchant. Great blue herons waded in the sandy shallows near the dock. Sneeze was at my side. Bear was asleep on the couch. The Catholics were playing card games. I sat on the screen porch alone that night and listened to the animals, wolves in the distance. The full moon, *madame*, a thunder moon, glowed on the horizon behind the red pine and slowly leaned across the entire narrows and bay. Millions of mosquitoes hummed to me on the screens. That was a night of ancient memories.

Sneeze was out at dawn, and his bark awakened me from a dream about my father, he was caught by heavy waves and vanished near Cemetery Island. Two skunks scurried away from the houseboat with some of our food. Sneeze was a reservation dog and wisely did not give chase. Marion came down to the dock, and we talked about skunks. The first beams of sunlight broke through the red pine and glanced across her face and the calm bay. The pungent scent of skunk lingered near the dock and houseboat. I was certain she wanted to talk with me about the priest, *madame*, but she could not find a way to break that silence of priestly manners. I wavered and said the priest and monk were very close, but at that very moment the monk walked down to the dock. Swayback pinched his nose over the scent of skunk. There was no chance for me to return to the subject of clerical crave and perversion. Marion seemed to understand, though, because she put her arm around me and told the monk to protect me from the evils of the world. Her stout body was warm and moist. Swayback laughed and said the church always protects altar boys from the evils of the outside world. He was right about that, *madame*, but that moment on the dock would bear no irony.

Suddenly a red floatplane roared out of the narrows just above the shoreline of the bay. Marion waved at the pilot in the open cockpit. She told me he was a retired psychiatrist who lived nearby in a summer cabin. I wanted to be a pilot, *madame*, at that very prescient moment of a psychiatric flyover. Patrick and the priest soon joined us on the dock that early morning. I did not want to leave. I wanted to live there the rest of my life, or at least the rest of the summer, but then, of course, my dear mother came to mind. She needed me to protect her from those nasty men. Marion prepared breakfast over a grill on the screen porch. Patrick placed his arm around my shoulder as we walked alone to the dock shortly after breakfast. Once again, *madame*, there was a crucial moment to talk about the priest, but candor and sincerity were overcome by hesitation and manners. Sneeze was the first aboard the houseboat. He ran to the bow, put his paws on the rail, barked and smiled. Marion waved to me, a tearful farewell. I knew that we would never meet again. I searched for her face at every turn, in every crowd, and about ten years later tried to locate her at Lake Namakan. The airborne psychiatrist died only months earlier at his cabin. The Ash River residents had no idea what had become of Patrick and Marion. I knew her for less than a day and yet was truly touched by her love and sensitivity. The Queen Marva slowly backed away forever that morning from the dock on Hoist Bay. Father Meme and Swayback waved from the bridge and then consecrated our departure with the sign of the cross.

Father Meme was at the helm that morning and steered the houseboat straight for Namakan Island near the border with Canada. The glacial island is one of the largest in the lake and directly north of Hoist Bay. The altar boy pirates were ready at the bow, the sea was calm, and the sun was brilliant on the wake. Queen Marva shivered as usual, but our clerical captain decided that the island of his desire was close enough, about two hours away at most, and there was no reason to strain the engines. Sneeze and the pirates leaned over the port bow and watched the wide cutwater crease the waves, a perfect trace of summer passage. We talked about swimming and how much colder the water was compared to the smaller lakes at home on the reservation. My father loved to swim, but when he was older his lungs and heart were not strong enough to survive the temperature and exertion. I imagined my father, *madame*, with me on the bow of the house-boat, the chief of the native pirates back from the war in Korea. I always have the right to imagine my father because he died so young. I saw his radiant face as the pilot of the pontoon airplane, and no doubt the psychiatrist would provide a clinical observation of my projections. My father is always with me, forever a native sense of perfect presence.

Was your father a soldier, *madame*, during the war? Really? The French Resistance? And then, as you told me earlier, he wrote for the newspaper *Combat*. Albert Camus has inspired many writers. I am one of them. Do you think he might travel with you the next time you visit? You are always welcome to stay at my house on the reservation.

Yes, back to the prurient adventures on the Queen Marva. Namakan Island was very large, probably three miles long, and it appeared at a distance to be the very shore of the entire lake. I turned from the bow and saw the priest and monk touching each other at the helm, and only then worried about the direction of the houseboat. The previous night had been so pleasant and by chance the altar boys were protected by the generosity of Marion and Patrick. Yes, *madame*, do you think she wanted to adopt me as they had lost a native daughter? On the second day, Swayback and the priest were much bolder about their sexual practices in front of the altar boys. I perceive and appreciate bears, mallards, humans, and other animals that are omnisexual, or pansexual teasers, but priests and monks vowed celibacy. Swayback and Father Meme, however, are moral criminals. The perfect punishment for the moral crimes of the priest is sacrifice. The altar boys turned away from the sexual spectacle on the bridge, but the pirates were not above the curious gaze. I looked past the voyeuristic scene and imagined a flyover by the psychiatrist as the priest was engaged in houseboat sex. Father Meme might respond that he was not in his vestments. I have used that psychiatrist flyover scene several times in my stories. Swayback shouted his name to the island, and then he sang popular songs: "I Believe" and "Doggie in the Window." Sneeze barked at him when he sounded the *arf arf* lyrics, and we moaned when he sang, "I do hope that doggie's for sale." Namakan Island suddenly loomed near the starboard bow. The island was enormous, a rocky shoreline thick with birch and red and white pine. Father Meme worried about a place to dock the houseboat. Swayback took over the helm because the priest was much too nervous, an unstable captain. His command of cars and boats was jerky. The sun was almost overhead, and a slight breeze came out of the east, a reverse of the wind direction overnight was a common signature of a storm on the reservation. The sky was perfectly clear, bright blue, not a trace or streamer of clouds. The monk slowed the boat as we came close to the island. The priest found nothing on the lake map that would indicate a secure moorage. The shoreline was lush, moody, ancient, and rocky. The west side of the island was too risky to moor the houseboat. Swayback decided to slowly maneuver the boat close to the shore and circle the island in search of a sandy bay. Queen Marva trembled slightly near the rocky shore, but the boat was almost silent at the lowest speed. The cutwater hardly creased the dark water around Namakan Island. There was evidence of a beaver lodge near a creek. The narrow birch had incisor tooth marks near the ground, about the height of a beaver. The beaver are nocturnal, secretive, and observed only with great concentration. Sometimes at twilight you can hear the mews of the kit beavers. The houseboat slowly continued along the south shore and then turned north near the international border.

Perhaps it would be easier, *madame*, to show you the location of the island on our napkin map. So, here is the outline of the lake, a few islands, the international border, and Namakan Island. There, at a point on the southeast shore of the island, two bald eagles landed in a huge nest high in a white pine. The boat moved silently along the shore. The eagles spread their wings and arose from the nest, soared over the trees, turned, glided lower, skimmed just above the calm surface of the lake, caught a small fish, and returned to the nest. We could see two gray eaglets stretch their necks, ready to fly. I told the priest and the monk that eagles always cut a sprig of white pine for the nest, a natural scent that heals and protects the eaglets. The priest mocked my enthusiasm for the eagles, and the monk said sometimes he carries a dandelion sprig in his pocket. The altar boys were disgusted, to say the least, by the crudity and insensitivity of the priest and monk. They pretended to be godly and mannered overnight for dinner and a secure moorage, but that was never their true character. The boat almost circled the entire island, and then on the north shore the monk slowly turned into a small bay with a sandy shoreline, a perfect natural moorage. Wigwam Point was the name on the map, and the bay was encircled by mighty red pines. The breeze teased an ancient sound in the branches. The Queen Marva slowly came ashore on the smooth sand. Sneeze was the first in the water. He ran ahead to the shore, turned, and waited for the altar boys. The sand was hot in the bright sun. The air was moist, and the breeze carried a rich scent of pine that late morning. We explored the nearby woods and rocky shore, and then returned to the boat for lunch. We were so excited by the island that we almost forgot about food. We ate apples, cheese, crackers, and peanut butter on the upper deck. We pretended the houseboat was ours, and we were native voyageurs. Father Meme and the monk were already in the double bed, naked, and tangled together in rampant sex. The natural world, beaver, muskrat, kingfishers, bald eagles, *madame*, were always more exciting and memorable than the sleazy, depraved practices of the mission priest and his toady monk.

The Altar Boy War was declared by three adolescent warriors, *oshkinawewi ogichidaa*, in a ceremony late that afternoon, Tuesday, July 28, 1953, at Namakan Island. The altar boys marched

---

deep into the woods after crackers and cheese to conspire against the wicked priest and the singer swayback from the monkery. We were much wiser and stronger by innate reason in the natural world than by the perverse liturgy of the mission priest or any heavenly precepts of monotheism and salvation. Father Meme scared me at the altar and confessional more than any dream or fantastic nightmare beast has ever done. He tried to chase the true nature out of my reason, and he tried to pervert the imagination and memories of my father. His bloody nose and sleazy sexual rage were fearsome. Pants and Bear were hired as altar boys about a month before me, and they barely survived the lecherous fury of the priest. Pants, first, and then Bear told me they were pushed once or twice a week into the shrouded confessional and commanded to masturbate with the priest. Pants said the priest sucked on his penis. One of my odious duties, as you know, *madame*, was to clean the blood and semen on the bench of the narrow confessional. You are generous to appreciate the risky cause of our conspiracy to torment, bedevil, and then sacrifice the wicked priest. The altar boys declared war that afternoon under the white pine to trick the priest and monk into erotic animal positions, those described in the *Manabosho Curiosa*, then abandon them nude on the island. Later we would tease and torment the priest at the mission by red dyes in the holy water and protective canvas on the bench in the confessional. We soured the sacramental wine with horseradish, cut the laces of his shoes, and substituted the pictures of young men on his chest of drawers with pictures of a bear, raven, and a dog behind the wheel of a car suited in clerical vestments. That, *ma chère madame*, would be only the start of the Altar Boy War.

Swayback had already prepared dinner, baked beans, canned ham, and pineapple when we returned to the houseboat. He cooked the entire meal, including the pineapple, over an open fire on the beach. The scent of pork and beans wafted deep into the woods and surely inspired the bears, wolves, and skunks. I have never forgotten the exact details of that meal because that was the start of our war, so intense and determined, and the first strategic maneuver against the priest and monk. Father Meme was nude, already drunk on gin, and leaning over the bow of the boat. Swayback waved to the priest and sang a popular song. The sound of his voice was unseemly, out of tune with the nature of the island. He raised a spoon and lowered his voice: "Every time I hear a newborn baby cry, or touch a leaf or see the sky, then I know why, I believe." Sneeze moaned and moved to the shady side of the beach. There was a slight, warm breeze, and the sun touched the high branches of the white pine. Father Meme waded to the beach, a contrary rosy beast, and his penis was hidden in a thicket of curly red hair. I mentioned the curiosa and teased him to pretend he was mounting a bear. He hunched over, thrust his penis, moved his head from side to side, and growled. Bear mocked the moves and then doubled over with laughter. Sneeze barked at the wild priest. I invited the monk to pose as a snow-shoe hare, and then a white tailed fawn ready to be mounted. Swayback was an eager player, aroused by the scenes from the curiosa, but then he stimulated his penis and pursued the altar boys. The war tease and mockery had become a perverse reality. Pants ran into the woods to escape the sexual rage. The priest shouted obscene curses and wagged his rosy penis. Bear swam into the bay. Father Meme pursued him into the water, but the priest could not swim. I shouted the first liturgy that came to mind from the sacraments, I baptize you in the name of the father and the son and the holy spirit, but that only inspired the lusty chase. That scene, *ma chère madame*, was our *naniizaanizi gakiiwe*, dangerous or panic portage. The rapid, panic beat of a metal spoon on a bean pot distracted the monk and confused the priest. The curiosa tease was not a wise maneuver, so we served the dinner on metal plates, and as we ate the spoons clanked louder. The priest circled the fire, unsteady, stumbled over the bean pot and slurred a song to the monk, "He pops, the boogie woogie rag, the chattanoogie shoe shine boy." He mumbled the word *boy* several times and then toppled over in the sand. The gin washed the hair on his chest. The altar boys enacted the second strategy of the war. Bear shouted that everyone must run nude on the beach. Pants wanted to dance nude in the light of the full moon. The priest moaned and mumbled the sacraments of his own penance as the white pine shadows covered his thick woozy body. The monk was aroused once again by the enticements of the altar boys. You must appreciate, *madame*, our war strategies teased the carnal, the only tactic that could sidetrack the clergy long enough to capture the Queen Marva. Swayback leaned back in the sand close to the priest. The muted sunset vanished in the hollow of his back. He was moody, poked the fire with a stick, and told confessional stories about his swayback, how he was always teased in school and at the seminary. We threw our clothes over the bow of the houseboat and waited for the moon to rise. The priest and monk were naked, and their clothes were on the boat. We swam out into the bay, circled back, and silently climbed over the stern of the boat. Sneeze was already aboard. We waited there for the first shine of the moon and then started the engine. I was at the helm for the first time, *madame*, and thrust the power in reverse to escape the wicked priest. The houseboat moved slowly away from the beach. The monk was surprised, needless to say, and shouted at us to stop. Father Meme awakened, turned from side to side, and then stumbled into the water after the boat. His nose started to bleed, and blood ran down his chest over his penis. The blood stained the shoreline. Pants and Bear waved to the monk and priest only after we were certain the houseboat was a secure distance from the shallow bay. Sneeze barked at them from the upper deck. The Altar Boy War started on time by the rise of the moon, and the second maneuver, after the risky curiosa ruse, was underway. I turned the boat toward the north and then west, away from Namakan Island. The moon shivered on the twilight waves, only a light breeze. The altar boys had stolen a boat and abandoned the monk and priest to their wicked, naked fate on the island. I remember, *madame*, how pleased we were at the time by the thought that the priest would survive only by his sense of nature, not by his clerical perversions. We laughed at the thought that the priest and monk might die by outrageous sex on the island, and then the altar boys turned silent. I reduced the engine power and turned closer to the shoreline. The trees were massive, mysterious in the moonlight. Bear wondered about our direction and wanted to return to the friendly dock where we were moored on the first night. I was convinced Patrick and Marion would welcome us back, especially without clergy, but we were lost at sea. Pants tried to read the navigation map, to locate overnight moorage, and then we started to worry. You may wonder, *madame*, about the altar boys, but they never once thought about returning to the wicked priest on that sandy beach. We were pirates, ready to navigate the lake forever to avoid the priest and monk. The moon bounced on the water, and the reflection was broken only by faint waves. Liberty is always chancy and insecure, but that night was a perfect voyageur *liberté* on Lake Namakan. Then on the port bow we saw a light, not moonlight, but a faint glow in the trees. I turned the houseboat closer to the shore and slowly moved toward the light. Bear was rightly worried that we might crash into the rocky shore. He leaned over the bow and watched the water. Sneeze sat next to me at the helm. The sound of loons was magical around the lake, one wistful song answered by another. We were lost by night, but the loons created a complete sense of native presence. I would live forever on the lake only to hear the loons. Bear shouted that he saw a sandy bay. I cut the engine, turned toward the beach, and waited to hear the rush of sand on the steel hull, the same sound we heard at the island. The light was from a cabin near the bay.

Barba boarded the houseboat. His name was the first and only word the old man uttered at first sight, and about two hours later he voiced a second word, *Anatolia*. Neither word made any sense to me at the time, but the altar boys smiled anxiously. Sneeze even smiled at the old man. Obviously, *madame*, we had beached the houseboat on his property. He shined a flashlight in our faces, stared at me for the longest time, and then waved the altar boys to shore. He pointed in silence to his cabin on the rise above the bay. We marched on the narrow path toward the light, and that night we wondered if we had abandoned two perverts only to be captured by a third one named Barba. Sneeze assured me the old man was not a menace. We waited at the door of his cabin by fear and manners. The light inside his cabin was a single kerosene lantern, and the scent reminded me of my mother and the reservation. I was lonesome, *madame*, and worried that we might never again return home. Pants, as usual, declared that he was hungry. The old man cut several slices of hard bread and placed some dried meat on the rough table. The cabin was built with heavy rough hewn timber, the beams were at least eight inches square. The table and chairs were hand crafted, but that was not the time to ask the old man who built his cabin and the furniture. Collar, a tiny old man on the reservation, built houses with solid beams. He earned his nickname because he always wore shirts with no collars. Collar in mind and the scent of pine beams eased my worries for a few minutes. We ate the hard bread in silence, and the old man watched each of the altar boys, and at times he raised his right eyebrow. His hands were small, strong, and tanned by the sun. He tapped the table with his fingernails. His face was almost hidden by a huge, wild, white beard, and his black eyes watched every move of the altar boys. Finally he gestured with his hands, apparently an invitation to talk. I said we were grateful to find his light because we were lost. Bear said we were looking for a dock on Hoist Bay. I asked the old man if he knew Patrick and Marion, but he remained silent. He must know his neighbors on the lake, or maybe he was a weird hermit, a retired, wicked monk. I know you appreciate how worried we were at the time, *madame*, we might have landed in the house of another perverse clergy.

Anatolia, that was the second word he uttered, but nothing more for the rest of the night. Pants slept at the table. Bear moved to the corner of the cabin and slept on the floor. Sneeze sat with me against a huge beam in the center of the cabin. The old man watched me for hours. I slept for a short time, but he was always there at the table. I finally walked out of the cabin, and the old man followed me to the houseboat. I slept on a bunk under a mosquito net, and the old man must have slept in the main cabin.

I am from Anatolia, he told me early that morning, standing over the bunk. Sneeze smiled, and the old man touched our heads. I almost broke into tears because he was so gentle. Then he held my hands and smiled, a beautiful wrinkled face. He could have been my father, *madame*, my great uncle, or my grandfather. Barba was Greek, an immigrant from Anatolia. I learned much later that he was born in 1878 and barely escaped from the Armenian genocide. Barba retired as a cobbler when his wife died, and moved to his cabin to live alone for the rest of his life. Patrick and Marion were two of his close friends on Lake Namakan. Obviously he knew we were in trouble, for how often do three boys run ashore in a houseboat? Barba waited in silence that night to hear our stories. Over breakfast the altar boys told him about the mission, the perversions of the priest and monk. Bear was very specific about sleazy sex practices and then turned away. I doubt that he wanted to hear that much about priestly sexual abuse from adolescent altar boys, *madame*, and he probably thought our stories were overstated if not fantastic. Actually, as you know, our stories were understated, but even at that an ordinary person would find the accounts hard to believe. Barba was very concerned that the priest and monk had been abandoned overnight on Namakan Island. The Altar Boy War was about vengeance, not about concern for the nasty clergy, and we were not worried about the number of animals and mosquitoes that might have discovered their wicked bodies. Barba was not pleased by our hatred, and he encouraged us to return to rescue the priest and monk on the island. Never, never, never! we shouted at the old man. Pants started to shiver at the mere mention of the clergy. Bear wanted to start the engines of the houseboat and leave the bay. Barba was sympathetic, but he was not persuaded by our stories of vengeance and war. Finally he appreciated our fear, if not our sense of shame, and decided that he would command the houseboat and rescue the priest and monk. Barba convinced the altar boys that he would report the sexual abuse to the county sheriff and notify the Roman Catholic Archbishop of Minnesota.

Barba was at the helm and turned the houseboat into the sandy bay near Wigwam Point. The beach was stained with the blood of the priest. Metal utensils were on the beach, but there was no sign of the priest or monk. Barba shouted several times to the priest and monk by name. Finally we heard a weak response, a mere whimper from the rocky woods. Sneeze cocked his ear and barked at the moan in the trees. Swayback was the first to appear on the beach, his face, eyes, and body swollen by mosquito bites. He was recognizable only by the hollow of his back. He shuffled across the sand and could hardly speak because his lips were bloated. The altar boys were not sympathetic. He was naked, and we did not want to touch his body. Barba opened the starboard gate and helped the monk to a bed in the cabin. Swayback rightly avoided our eyes. Minutes later the priest came out of the woods, puffy and bloated by hundreds of mosquito bites. His shoulders and thighs were scratched by the underbrush but not bloody. Father Meme scowled as he climbed aboard and stared at the altar boys with his evil blue eyes. Barba held out his hand, a friendly gesture. The priest pushed him aside and marched to the cabin.

The priest and monk were asleep by the time the houseboat moved away from the bay and set a course for the Ash River. Barba told us haunting stories as the boat passed Cemetery Island. His cabin is nearby, and on summer nights of the new moon he has heard native voices and songs. Some nights there were great celebrations. Many unwitting campers have been driven from the island by the voices. The island is even more dangerous in the winter, when native spirits enchant skiers and snowshoers to rest in the snow. Those who are seduced by the voices of the spirits, and lean back to rest in the snow, never return. Barba said the bodies are found in the spring, always against a snow bank or stone, asleep with an eternal smile. The priest and monk were awake by the time the houseboat turned from the lake into the channel to the Ash River. Barba slowed the boat, reversed the engine at just the right moment, and hardly bumped the dock. Sneeze was the first to leave the boat. He danced and barked on the dock. Barba told the rental agent to contact the local county sheriff. Some time later the priest and monk were clean and dressed, but swollen, and ordered meals at the Ash River Restaurant. Father Meme, always wicked and wily, told the owners that the altar boys had stolen the houseboat and left them without food or water overnight on Namakan Island. The waitress was sympathetic, and the story spread quickly that the three altar boys were reservation natives and had abused the priest and a disabled monk and stolen their clothes and money. By the time the sheriff arrived at the scene, the story had already become a certainty at the Ash River Restaurant. Barba told the sheriff about the altar boys, the stories of abuse, but the priest had already implicated the old man as an accomplice to the crimes. Barba was an honorable man, never doubted by his good neighbors, always trusted by the sheriff and the lake community, but the priest was more persuasive because the boys were reservation natives. The sheriff clearly trusted the old man but thought he was credulous and unwary. Father Meme appeared to be reliable, *madame*, because he conveyed the sacraments, and natives were criminals by shame, culture, and reservation. Minutes later the priest had a bloody nose over his lunch. Swayback handed the priest a napkin. Father Meme made a bloody sign of the cross and prayed for the salvation of the altar boys. Our treacherous panic portage, *naniizaanizi gakiiwe*, would never end until that priest was sacrificed. The altar boys were forsaken once more, and the owner of the restaurant turned away from the natives. Sneeze was shooed from the restaurant, and the owner refused to serve lunch to the altar boys.

Bagidenjige

The Altar Boy War was almost lost, as you know, at the Ash River Restaurant. The next maneuver was on the mission front, a strategic switch of priestly pictures. We substituted the picture of Pope Pius XII, Father Marcial Maciel, and Legionaries of Christ on the chest of drawers with a picture of Sneeze, vested to the nines in a black cassock and bone cross necklace. Father Meme did not notice the picture for several weeks, or else he ignored the picture of the canine driver at the wheel of his station wagon. Gorgeous prepared the spectacular scene, my mother made the priestly vestments, and our cousin took the pictures. Sneeze could not resist the notice. He seemed to appreciate the casual ironic pose with one paw on the steering wheel. He was serious, *madame*, but even so you could detect a smile in the picture. Sneeze heard the stories about mongrel chauffeurs, and he was always ready to drive. Father Meme scorned the stories about dog drivers on the reservation, but his churlish manner about native stories, mainly *naanabozho* trickster stories, was predictable. The priest cursed the *anishinaabe* word *animosh*, or dog, and any word for an animal. Surely, *madame*, you are not surprised that some dogs drive cars and even school buses. Sneeze actually first learned how to drive with me in a bumper car at the county fair.

The Animosh Driver School was established on the reservation more than eighty years ago with a generous endowment from a prosperous patron. Amelia White, the eccentric daughter of Horace White, once the editor of the *Chicago Tribune*, was enchanted by native animal stories and was convinced that dogs were not only prescient and loyal companions but could do most things better than humans. Gorgeous told me she was a prominent breeder of Afghan hounds and Irish wolfhounds. Amelia trained her animals to be warriors and military drivers, and they served in Dogs for Defense during the Second World War. Truly, *madame*, she trained many dogs to drive. Some detractors, especially those who envied her wealth, were convinced that she hired a mongrel chauffeur. Many of the hound warriors were buried with honors, and you can read the grave markers in a memorial cemetery at the School of American Research in Santa Fe, New Mexico. Slyboots, a distant cousin of my grandmother, was a healer, teaser, and great storier on the reservation. Amelia was truly healed by his humor and convinced by his tricky stories that many reservation dogs were already drivers, and with more training could be reliable chauffeurs. Slyboots pointed out the obvious, that many dogs move directly behind the steering wheel once the driver leaves the car. Now, *madame*, evidence of the story is clearly by the manner of the dogs. Not every dog would be a driver. Some dogs stay in the back seat, always content as passengers. Most driver dogs move to the front seat at every chance, and they wait at the wheel ready to drive. Have you noticed that the driver dogs seldom look a passerby straight in the eye. Why? Well, *madame*, because bystanders might only see the face of a dog, not a driver. Some dogs actually look a stranger right in the eye, pant and smile, always friendly and proud to be employed as a dog chauffeur on the reservation or in the city. Slyboots trained more than a hundred reliable *animosh* chauffeurs for priests, anthropologists, government agents, tourists, hunters, widows, and others on the reservation. He negotiated fair contracts for the drivers that provided good salaries, regular meals, wild vacation time, and comfortable accommodations with suitable uniforms. Construction companies hired sturdy dog drivers, and schoolchildren wanted *animosh* school bus drivers. Amelia was moved by the outcome of her endowment to train dog drivers, a prosperous new enterprise on the reservation. Slyboots was truly a wizard, a natural healer and persuasive storier, but he could not convince the insurance companies to provide coverage for *animosh* drivers. Amelia never anticipated the righteous wrath of animal protection crusaders, especially those from England. The Animosh Driver School was accused of abuse and misuse of animals. Dog drivers, the early crusaders declared, were exposed to unproductive stress and toxic exhaust on the highways. Slyboots agreed to endorse the first union of dog drivers, but the animal crusaders would not be dissuaded by a mere labor union. The actions and protests of these crusaders, mostly women, were reported widely in magazines and newspapers. Mike Wallace surely would have covered a dog driver story, *madame*, but this event was long before his time as a journalist. The actual dog drivers, mostly male, were worried that the crusaders were devious and exploited the labor and liberty of dog drivers for other political reasons, such as suffrage. The contest reached the state legislature for consideration at the very same time an *animosh* chauffeur for a district school had a minor accident near the capitol. The driver of the other car, a local pharmacist, was astounded to meet a wolfish mongrel with a valid reservation driver license. The insurance company revoked the vehicle coverage for the school district, and that convinced the legislature to vote against dog drivers. The animal crusaders continued the holy war, but they soon altered the cause to rescue reservation cats and dogs from bad weather. The Animosh Driver School closed that summer, more than eighty years ago. Slyboots observed that the new state law prohibiting dog drivers said nothing in the fine print about *animosh* pilots. Amelia White, as you might expect, came to the rescue a second time with an endowment to train reservation pilots at the Animosh Ultralight Pilot School.

The Roman Catholic Archbishop of Minnesota never received a complaint about the sexual abuses of Father Meme. The Archdiocese reported no record of a priest by that name. Barba, the old man who persuaded the altar boys to rescue the priest and monk, reported the nickname of the priest, as he was not aware of any other name. So, several months later the old man visited the reservation. He was concerned about the way the altar boys had been treated at the Ash River Restaurant. Barba and Gorgeous became immediate friends, as you can imagine, and, naturally, they told stories about the altar boys. Gorgeous said his name was Barba Gerasimo. Shelter took many pictures. There, on the mantel, *madame*, is a picture of the altar boys, Barba, Gorgeous, and Sneeze. The sexual abuse report was moot by fact, duty, and action because the archdiocesan hierarchy would have denied any accusations of sexual abuse and protected a priest by any name, Father Meme or Conan Whitty. The wicked priest was invulnerable, *madame*, and forever saved from criminal prosecution. Only some saints, demons, stray priests, certain spies, and presidents enjoy such aegis, patronage, and absolute immunity. Surely you can appreciate that sacrifice was the only remedy.

I am very pleased, *ma chère madame*, that you kindly accepted the invitation to visit my house. As you can see, the entire structure is handcrafted from plantation Douglas fir logs. The shape of the logs is natural, and nothing is milled or lathed. Barba built a similar cabin at Lake Namakan, but he squared the beams from local timber. Most of my electrical power comes from solar panels, and from a new sustainable methane generator, probably the first one on the reservation. Please, *madame*, sit near the bay windows with a view of Wiindigoo Lake. The name in *anishinaabe* means monster or winter cannibal, but the priests and state cartographers contend the true name is Mission Lake. The Archdiocese lobbied the geological survey for an ecclesiastical name, but natives bear a sense of natural presence. Father Meme, as you know, was sacrificed in an ice house on Wiindigoo Lake. I presume, *madame*, that you would like the usual, Hendrick's Gin? Twice served, and this distinctive gin is evermore customary. Yes, my parents were born here, and my father built a cabin on the rise south of the Indian Mission Church of the Snow.

Marcial Maciel is featured twice in the framed pictures on the chest of drawers at the mission. First as a handsome sixteen-year-old boy at about the time he was inspired to become a priest, and in the second picture he and about fifty young Legionaries of Christ are with Pope Pius XII at the Vatican. Father Marcial Maciel Degollado was born in Mexico and ordained as a priest about three years after he founded the Legionaries of Christ in January 1941. Father Maciel became a maestro of congregations. He was inspired, ambitious, a premier sexual abuser of seminarians, and always protected by the Holy See in Vatican City. Father Maciel, you see, raised millions of dollars for the Roman Catholic Church. The altar boys were not aware of this congregation at the time, but later we learned that one of those in attendance was Father Meme. No doubt the priest learned some of his kinky sexual practices in the company of Father Maciel and the Legionaries of Christ. Sixty some years later he was accused of sexual abuse of seminarians. He molested young men in his care, and within a few miles of the Vatican. Yes, you are right to inquire, *madame*, about my sources of this information. I do not mean to be evasive, but would you like another drink? Please join me, one more gin and tonic before our surprise dinner.

The *National Catholic Reporter* covered part of the story once the case was rescued and reconsidered by the Vatican. The *Hartford Courant* reported on the sexual abuse of clergy and the exposé of Father Maciel. *The Vows of Silence* by Jason Berry and Gerald Renner provided the most serious and complete investigative reports on the testimony and allegations of nine men against Father Maciel. Catholic seminarians and many adolescent boys, about the same age as the altar boys at the mission, were seduced, sexually manipulated, and masturbated by the sleazy priest. Some of the boys remembered the "grooming rituals," which, according to the authors, was a common practice of pedophiles.

Jason Berry noted that Father Maciel told some of the callow seminarians that because of chronic pain, a swollen prostate, for instance, he was given permission, a special dispensation for sex by Pope Pius XII. Father Maciel told some of the needy boys that Jesus Christ put a cross on his shoulders, and such pain must be treated by masturbation. Father Maciel was found guilty of sexual abuse, but there was no canonical or criminal prosecution of the documented accusations. The priest, in a sense, was exonerated of his crimes. Father Maciel was once encouraged, favored, and praised by Pope John Paul II.

Now, *madame*, our surprise dinner is about to be delivered by Pierre Hertel de Beaubassin and the Mayagi Ashandiwin Restaurant. My surprise was actually very easy because the chef is one of your great admirers. Pierre might deliver dinner to me alone only if my legs were broken. He is generous but not always sympathetic about disabled journalists. So, should we eat at the table near the window and watch the sunset over Wiindigoo Lake? Pierre brought us a sampler of the entrées we ordered early in the week. My personal contribution to dinner is a fine bottle of Châteauneuf du Pape Cuvée de Mon Aïeul.

Futurity, *ma chère madame, à votre santé.*

Gorgeous is a teaser, and his teases arise by natural reason, that is, he pushes names and images, distinctions and turns of irony, back to the natural world. He told me the water ouzel and river otter swim like fish but never pose as salmon. Yes, *madame*, his tropes are obscure, but not to the wild rainbow trout. The pleasures of his native tease are the practices of survivance, that sense of resistance and native presence. Gorgeous presented each of the altar boys with a necklace, a string of empty, spent rifle shells.

Pants could not decide what to do with the necklace because it was too heavy to wear around his neck. Bear examined each shell on the necklace, and then wore it around his shoulder. I had no idea what the necklace should mean, or the caliber of the casing, and worried that my great uncle would expect me to account for these details. You see, *madame*, the presentation was a tease, but a serious one because the necklace was the same as the one worn by the distinguished warrior, Hole in the Day. Gorgeous told me to wear the necklace at services, the ironic beads of a native rosary. He created the necklaces and teased us to be warriors and to learn about the *anishinaabe* war with the United States Army. The Pillager warrior Bugonaygeshig, or *bagone giizhig*, translated as Hole in the Day, collected hundreds of Krag Jorgensen army rifle shells in his garden at Sugar Point on Leech Lake. Third Infantry Christian soldiers fired the bullets at natives, but only the soldiers died on October 5, 1898. The army casualties were eleven wounded and six dead, including Major Melville Cary Wilkinson, a veteran of the Civil War. The major probably had a death wish, *madame*, as there was no reason for him to stand in the line of fire. Hole in the Day was arrested a few days earlier by federal marshals because he refused to testify in court. He escaped with about twenty warriors, and the marshals called for immediate military assistance. A company of immigrant soldiers arrived and boarded steamers to the cabin owned by Hole in the Day at Sugar Point. The Pillager warriors were outnumbered more than three to one by the soldiers, and yet, *madame*, the elusive natives won the war in a single day. Clearly, there was never a plausible reason to declare war on the Pillagers. The warriors easily defeated the inexperienced soldiers, who had no cause to fight natives. Hole in the Day returned to his cabin a few days later. His mature vegetable garden was in ruins, covered with foxholes, and sacred ceremonial objects had been stolen by the military from his cabin. Gorgeous wanted the altar boys to remember that war and become warriors by the tease of the necklace. By that he seemed to mean that we should learn the enemy way and fight for survivance over victimry. The Altar Boy War was the start of our practice as warriors.

Now that was another delicious, memorable dinner. Yes, *madame*, much better here than at the restaurant. I truly wish you could stay longer on the reservation. The tribal council is very impressed by your knowledge and integrity. Thank you for the invitation, *madame*, perhaps next spring in Paris. Look, the last moths bounce at the window, determined as ever to make our night their day. Turn out the lights, and the instant resistance at the window is over for the moths, but not for me. I too have been obsessed by light, by stained glass church windows, the glorious music in Saint John's Abbey Church. The priest and monk tried to turn out my vision at the window, my ecstasy. The full moon is a natural decoration in the red pine, and the moon bounces on the waves. There, listen, the sounds of the loons in the autumn are more wistful and memorable than at any other time of year. This, *madame*, is a perfect sense of native presence. I was a journalist for a daily newspaper for more than thirty years, as you know, but could never again live in the city. The natural sounds and turn of seasons are ordinary songs that heal the heart. French voyageurs and fur traders, our ancient relatives, discovered a natural paradise in the northern woodland and glacial lakes. Empire politics aside for a moment, the nature of these beautiful, mysterious lakes and mighty pine trees have touched and united the hearts and memories of voyageurs and natives for more than ten generations, some three centuries. Now, *madame*, would you like a cappuccino?

Roman Nishiwe was a real native warrior on the reservation. He was mum most of the time, and he always carried a rifle over his shoulder, at the public health hospital, the federal school, and even in the line at the ice cream store. The old man was a natural sniper, a deadeye shooter even as a boy, and he served with my great uncle in the First World War. His surname was a nickname. The word *nishiwe* in translation means "kill people." The altar boys wanted to hear his warrior stories, but we were naturally hesitant to even mention his name. Gorgeous intervened, as they were close friends, and we were invited to his cabin on the north side of Wiindigoo Lake. Nishiwe was an altar boy for the first immigrant priest at the mission, Father Fusco. Sneeze was very cautious on the narrow rocky portage near his cabin. Four rather nasty mongrels circled and barked. The old deadeye sniper met us outside with a huge, toothless, empty smile. Nishiwe teases strangers with his rosy gums. He pinched the muscles on our shoulders, and then pushed us one by one into the tiny cabin. The altar boys sat on benches around a metal counter that had been discarded at the hospital. Pants said he was hungry. The old man polished the table with his sleeve, and then he caught my eye. He reached into a cast iron stove and produced a box of graham crackers. I was entranced by his stories about the war at Sugar Point. He was an altar boy at the time and remembers the soldiers in blue uniforms on the steamers, the crack of rifle shots, and a day later the bloody vegetable garden. The bold warriors climbed the fence and taunted the soldiers, but there were no native casualties. Nishiwe picked only the wounded cucumbers on the wooden fence. He told me he was touched forever by the *midewiwin* ceremonies of the great warrior Hole in the Day. His grandfather was a singer at the *midewiwin*, the native medicine dance. Father Fusco warned the altar boy he would be shamed by the great savior if he continued to dance with the devil. Nishiwe laughed and told me the priest was always wary of native healers. His cabin, *madame*, was a tiny nest, one room, crowded with mongrels, and covered with tarpaper. His stories about native warriors and snipers were evasive, always turned to situations, to conversations with ancestors, the seasons and weather at the moment, and then he would gesture to his mongrels. Sneeze moved closer to the old man, almost covered his bare feet. Tease a warrior, *madame*, and never cower to the enemy. Nishiwe told me that, and then he laughed. The old warrior gestured to the altar boys to follow him across the room. He laughed again, because the room was so small, about twelve altar boy steps across. In the corner he uncovered a heavy wooden cabinet with two sizable locks. Nishiwe turned in silence and created a sense of suspense as he slowly unlocked the cabinet. He looked back to the mongrels and altar boys, and then revealed the secret treasure of a sniper. There were seven rifles locked in the cabinet. Gorgeous told the old man about the necklaces, and he was ready to show us the actual army rifle, a Krag Jorgensen. Bear caught his breath as he held the rifle in his hands. The gun was heavy, and the parts, bolt action and stock, were clean and polished with fine machine oil. The old warrior was devoted to his store of weapons. He fired and cleaned them at least once a week. I raised the rifle, aimed at a knot on the beams, and imagined the immigrant soldiers who carried the same weapons at Sugar Point.

The war, *madame*, was actually started by an accidental discharge of a Krag Jorgensen. Nishiwe always carried a Winchester Model 1894, the same lever action rifle most of the natives used against the Third Infantry at Sugar Point. One by one the old warrior presented his cache of weapons. The Winchester Model 70 was the only rifle in his cabinet that had a telescopic sight. I knew that was the weapon he used as a sniper, but later he confided in me that he used a rifle with an ordinary iron sight. Naturally, he expected me to ask him why he did not use the weapon with the telescopic sight. I would not continue in this manner, *madame*, if you had not expressed a strong interest in the technical aspects of the sniper story. First, though, we must have ice wine for dessert, Bonny Doon Muscat Vin de Glaciere, from a winery near Santa Cruz, California. Gorgeous and Nishiwe served in the First World War, as you know, and they returned with a taste for good wine from France. Regularly they drove to the city to find imported wine and shared every bottle over stories about the women of France. Not stories about the war, but the women. They would be here tonight, to meet you, and savor this ice wine. Nishiwe told me he read about one of the most deadly snipers in history, Simo Häyhä, from Finland. The sniper used ordinary iron sights and earned the nickname White Death because he wore winter camouflage and killed more than five hundred soldiers of the Soviet Union. The use of an iron sight concentrates an innermost sense rather than the precise point of a target. Similarly a slingshot is by concentration, reactive meditation, not a mere target point. The telescopic sight, however, is essential for specific, secure shots that torment the target, close but not deadly. Nishiwe handed me the Winchester Model 70, a perfectly balanced weapon.

Nishiwe once trained native warriors to be snipers, a secret society on the reservation. He also trained snipers for the United States Marine Corps. I heard many rumors about this society, but not one specific story. No one was ever named as a sniper or warrior, and no event or extreme course of action was ever attributed to the society. I heard the word *bagidenjige*, to ease the mind, release ideas, and hold a funeral, in connection with the society. That word and description, however, has never been mentioned in a story. The altar boys assumed the notion of secret warriors to concoct our strategies and maneuvers against the priest. Nishiwe taught me that autumn how to be a sniper of torment, close, closer but never deadly. I wanted to be a secret warrior the first time he showed me how to estimate the windage and distance of a target by the telescopic sight on the Winchester Model 70. Gorgeous told me that the secret warriors met only once or twice a year to resolve investigations and the perusal of native targets. So, the altar boys decided to meet every week to compare tactics and targets at the mission.

The sniper warriors work alone and in their own time. Nishiwe told me that snipers never leave a trace of their presence. So, how would they create a sense of native presence? Presumably, a secret presence created by the actions of snipers. I was told, *madame*, that several snipers are native women, inspired, no doubt, by Major Lyudmila Pavlichenko, the great Russian sniper who killed more than three hundred German soldiers and many enemy snipers during the Second World War. I was an altar boy warrior, and sniper, as you know, but my stealth and sub-rosa maneuvers would never earn access to the *anishinaabe* secret society of snipers and warriors. I encountered only one warrior sniper, and that was by chance. I was a journalist writing about corruption at native casinos and interviewed a casino manager who was about to be indicted on charges of fraud and embezzlement. The manager was murdered the next morning, apparently by a sniper. He was shot at a great distance in a hotel room, through a narrow opening of a sliding balcony door. The sniper waited for the manager to come out of the shower. The bullet passed through the sheer curtain, a thick white towel, his heart, and the heavy hallway door. The secret warrior revealed an indirect trace of circumstantial evidence, a potential story. I was at the casino that night and decided to pose as a warrior sniper, a fantasy of my time as an altar boy at the mission. I imagined the scenes, pretended to be the enemy, and investigated the scene as a sniper. I observed the warrior a few days later in my imaginative sight as a sniper. Three casino executives were murdered that month. I noticed the very same person on video surveillance tapes on each night of an assassination. She played three different games, but only casually. Most gamblers play the same casino games, but the warrior played a counter-pattern, the pose of apathy. She did not want to be seen at the same game because she might be recognized. The sniper warrior apparently observed the movements of each casino executive and then prepared the death shot. I was a sniper that night and would have considered a similar strategy. I followed her to the restaurant, watched her moves to learn the enemy way, and, uninvited, sat at her table. She smiled and was not concerned. No, *madame*, the scene was not at our sunset table. The casino and reservation were in another state. I introduced myself as a native warrior and journalist, but she remained unnamed, not even a simulated nickname for the casino moment. I noticed the slightest tic in one eye and felt certain that she was the sniper. I imagined her stealth and sniper moves as a warrior, the three casino assassinations, and revealed my observations in stories. She smiled, and then calmly embellished the accounts she had just heard. The fantastic conclusions of her counterstories were perfect evasions. The sniper warrior is never drawn into other stories. She was brilliant, *madame*, no sensible person would connect the fantastic stories to actual crimes. Whatever you write, she told me, must be fantastic. Later that night the last indicted casino executive, a tribal leader, was found dead in a hotel bathroom, shot three times in the chest. The sniper once again secured a sight and fired through an open balcony door. A perfect pattern of bullets passed through the bathroom wall and entered the chest of the old man as he sat on the toilet. She was more potent than many celebrated war snipers. I wrote several investigative stories about casino corruption and the four unsolved assassinations. I wrote about the warrior sniper in second person, a feature story. You observe the target, investigate the opportunities, and leave no casual, personal, perceptible cause or trace of presence. Yes, indeed, *madame*, the same second person narrative as in *The Fall* by Albert Camus. I used the second person narrative only once since then, and that in an investigative story about the proscribed, covert, domestic operation and location of the Central Intelligence Agency. I received a picture postcard of the Sistine Chapel a few weeks later, with a printed note, Tricky stories of an altar boy sniper. How would she know about me? The return address was The Holy See, Vatican City.

The altar boys continued their usual ritual duties at Mass and other services. Father Meme was wary. He stared, grunted his words in the morning, and then later tried to be friendly. His nosebleeds increased, two or three times a week, and regularly in the confessional. Sometimes he would track blood from the booth to his residence at the back of the mission church. I could not escape his nasty, bloody presence. My most miserable duties, as you know, were cleaning the priestly blood and semen from the confessional. The priest was always dangerous, and we were resolute, tenacious, and determined to drive him from the mission. The altar boys decided on more severe maneuvers in our war against the bloody priest. Father Meme was treacherous, smarmy, unbearable, and yet he never contained his needy lust for the altar boys.

Nishiwe was eager to train me to be a sniper. Two or three times a week he tied wooden silhouettes in the trees, close and afar, and told me to imagine the priest, to concentrate only on the target, the motion of the subject, not the sight. He taught me to anticipate as a predator every motion of the priest, and to sense his presence by meditation, not by mere distance. Sneeze was alert, and his nose moved with every sound. The ravens strutted and rolled over on the nearby rocks. I concentrated on one silhouette and squeezed the trigger between heartbeats. The ravens bounced and croaked at me. Nishiwe directed me to hold my concentration on the motion of the silhouette and then shoot twice more in the same place. He was clearly not pleased by my show of enthusiasm and turned away. There were three bullet holes about an inch apart. I quickly learned to contain the excitement of my simulated executions of the priest. Nishiwe once painted a priestly figure on the silhouette with an erect penis. I rapidly shot the ordained organ three times in a row, and the figure three times in the mock heart. Nishiwe allowed me to use his Winchester

Model 70, chambered for a 22 Hornet centerfire cartridge, and once he was convinced by my dedication, practice, and precision as a novice sniper, he loaned me the bolt action rifle for my war against the priest.

October was warm, bold, foxy, and the turn of colors, rosy hues. The birch and maple trees were a pure blush that year. Father Meme seemed to be more at ease, probably because the altar boys were more secure. We were concealed and confident of our mission. We continued our dedicated priestly service, and, at the same time, we conspired with deadly conviction to sacrifice the priest that winter after the celebration of Christmas. First, we were determined to coerce the priest by severe measures to leave forever the mission and the reservation. The priest could leave and live, or stay and be sacrificed. The altar boys traded misery notes in school, *madame*, and created Fourteen Torments for the priest based on the Fourteen Stations of the Cross. We became warriors by concentration on the ways of the enemy and by rigorous scrutiny, and we carefully staged the scenes of torment. We cautiously planned each maneuver, timed the actual series of moves, and tried to anticipate the rage of the priest, and, of course, how to prove our innocence of any conspiracy. Bear contrived fourteen crude, stained, wooden crosses that were placed at the site of each torment. The wood crosses were actually stained with the blood of the priest, from his nosebleeds in the confessional. The winter storms were early, cold and miserable, heavy snow, almost the first curse and torment. The altar boys set a sniper timetable. The Fourteen Torments commenced on weekdays in the first week of February 1954. The torments were not scheduled on Saturday or Sunday.

The First Torment was the most serious and risky. The altar boys condemned the priest to his first simulated death at the fish house. We wore shreds of white cloth as winter camouflage and waited that night in the red pine on a snowy rise near Wiindigoo Lake. Yes, *madame*, you can see it from here. The rise right over there, near the white pine. From there you could easily sight the fish house. I was in position with the borrowed rifle. Sneeze was at my side. Father Meme trudged to the fish house several times a week to masturbate over the hole in the ice. We waited for two nights, and finally he arrived in his heavy coat. I had already set the telescopic sight to a mark on the door. Pants estimated the precise position of the priest over the ice hole in the fish house. We knew his strict habits, moves, and positions. He would never stand between the door and cast iron stove. The two benches were on the other side near the fish hole. The priest was deceived by dedicated and dicey altar boy manners, *madame*, unaware of the intrigue and trickery, and, moved by his godless perversions, we were certain he would invite us to the fish house. We accepted only to calculate the precise sniper shots. He was so obsessed with sex and altar boys that he could not perceive his own menace. The priest once measured our penises in the mission residence. He told us that the bishop wanted accurate records on the altar boys. He mentioned those measures in the fish house and wanted to count our pubic hairs. Bear was the only altar boy who had a trace of hair, and so his nickname. Pants said he was hungry. Suddenly the priest was nude, his stout, erect penis bounced out of a tangle of red pubic hair. He leaned over the ice hole and masturbated. Bear measured the distance to the cast iron stove and marked the target on the door. Pants pointed at the priest and said, Away with him, crucify him. I shouted, Hail Mary, full of grace, the Lord is with thee, and then we ran fast away from the fish house.

I warmed my trigger finger and fired three rounds, the first maneuver of the Fourteen Torments. The bullets passed through the thin door in a tight circle on the mark and shattered the cast iron stove. Father Meme roared in a rage, ran nude out of the fish house, and looked in every direction. We covered our mouths to hold back the laughter and watched the rosy priest at a great, cold distance, a vindictive satire. I swear, *madame*, his evil eyes could ice a sunny heart. The altar boys ducked to escape the curse of his gaze. We were hidden by the deep snow and winter camouflage. Sneeze started to shiver, so we slowly backed away from the fish house on Wiindigoo Lake. Bear was out at dawn the next morning, hours before school, and as he nailed a red stained wooden cross over the fish house door, he noticed there were four bullet holes in the door. One hole was larger than the other three. Someone else must have been there and fired at the same time.

The Second Torment, much to our surprise, was enacted at the fish house the following night. The altar boys had not prepared for two sniper torments at the fish house, but the priest had invited the monk to visit and masturbate with him over the fish hole. Again, *madame*, the priest was so fascinated by sex with the monk that he lost his capacity to appreciate the danger. I fired three rapid shots and shattered the windows of the fish house. The priest roared and ran out nude as he had the previous night. Swayback breathed on his hands and danced around the fish house. The monk shivered, the priest was steamy. They returned to the fish house to masturbate. The altar boys were worried that the priest might find footprints, so we brushed over the snow back home. Gorgeous told me the priest was convinced the shooters were drunks from the village and never suspected the altar boys. Swayback was certain the altar boys were connected in some way, if not the actual shooters. The monk actually accused the altar boys after a funeral service. Father Meme refuted the notion, because he reasoned that natives were crafty thieves but not smart enough to be snipers. The priest was never aware of my secret training as a sniper warrior with Nishiwe. Bear nailed a second crude wooden cross over the door of the fish house and noticed once more that someone else had shot out the windows at the back of the fish house. Nishiwe might have been the second sniper, but the altar boys decided never to mention the situation.

The Third Torment was a maneuver with critical precision in the mission residence of the priest. The altar boys measured the position and distance from the outside entrance door to the chest of drawers. Pants waited near the mission residence for the priest to leave, and then he pushed the door open to determine the actual line of fire. I stretched out in the snow near the outhouse and focused the telescopic sight on the picture of Marcial Maciel, as a young man, and Pope Pius XII, surrounded by the Legionaries of Christ. Father Meme had burned the picture of Sneeze. Bear marked a target on the door, the exact line of fire to the pictures. The stars were brilliant, and the ice cracks thundered on the lake. Cold, cold, cold, *madame*, at twenty below zero the ice contracts, and a running crack sounds like thunder. The priest returned to the residence late that night. We marked time in the back of the warm mission church until we heard his return, the sound of his station wagon. Father Meme poured hot water into his huge copper bathtub for his warm, scented, nightly soakage.

Bear and Pants leaned back in the snow to watch the third torment of the priest. The rifle was in position. I focused the telescopic sight on the first target mark on the door, as we had at the fish house, fired one round, reloaded, shifted the sight slightly to the right mark, and fired a second round. The bullets entered the door about a foot apart and crashed through the two glass framed pictures. The priest roared and ran outside, his warm, wet body steaming in the cold air. Bear later nailed a wooden cross over the door of the mission residence. The priest burned the wooden cross in the morning. He had not yet discovered the two stained crosses nailed to the door of the fish house. Still, he did not suspect the altar boys as the shooters.

The Fourth Torment was one of the most pleasurable, if our sniper maneuvers can be so described at the mission. Father Meme was a regular visitor to the outside toilet, early every morning at the same time. His rituals were predictable, a breakfast of hard bread and cheese, coffee, and then to the crapper. Frequently, as the altar boys investigated his crapper practices, the priest would rush out of the mission residence straight to the outhouse in his bathrobe and untied boots. There, untouched by the extreme cold, he would likely read magazines and look at pictures of boys. Pants discovered that the priest collected issues of *Boys' Life* magazine, published by the Boy Scouts of America. The priest stored the magazines under his copy of the *Manabosho Curiosa*. The accurate inclination and direction of the bullet was even more critical than the sniper shots at the pictures on the chest of drawers. There was a slight risk that the priest, seated on the outside crapper, might lean to the right into the line of fire and be nicked or wounded in the right arm. The point of the torments was to scare the priest, but never at the altar or in the nave of the mission, and nothing deadly. Bear was under great pressure to measure the precise position, so he pretended to be the priest with a magazine. Bear grunted and moaned in the outhouse, and the altar boys bounced, laughed, and croaked like ravens. Early the next morning the altar boys stretched out behind a mound of snow, a safe distance from the back of the tatty outhouse, and counted the minutes by priestly routines. I considered the inclination and set the telescopic sight on the target mark and waited for the perfect moment to fire. Right on schedule the priest rushed to the outhouse in his undershirt and untied boots. His hot breath turned to clouds of ice crystals. The door spring squeaked and then slammed shut. Father Meme grunted on time. I leaned into the telescopic sight, concentrated on the presence of the priest, imagined the magazine in his thick, sweaty hands, envisioned the right moment, the actual course of the bullet, and then fired a single round. The bullet hit the target mark at the back of the outhouse and tore the pictures of boy scouts from his hands. The priest leaped from the crapper, charged through the door in a rage, and ran in wide circles around the outhouse. We erased our prints in the snow and backed away in camouflage. Bear nailed the fourth red stained wooden cross over the door of the outside toilet.

The Fifth Torment was a maneuver of everlasting humor and sniper trickery. Bear told the story about how the priest arrived at the mission that summer with smutty erotica and an enormous copper bathtub. Nightly he heated the water and soaked his rosy body in the huge container. Once or twice a month his bloody nose stained the scented bath water. My mother saw the evidence in the morning, the bloody water drained near our ancestors in the mission cemetery. His bloody bath in winter tinted the snow. The bathtub was located in an alcove of the mission residence. The only sight on the bathtub was through a high window. Pants told the priest he was hungry, and then waited in the residence to open the high window at the right moment. Father Meme invited the altar boys to his residence, but not that night. Come what may, he was always ready for chance sex and masturbation. I braced the rifle in the crotch of a white pine near the mission and waited on the priest, bath water, and window. The strategy was to fire three times at the side of the copper bathtub as the priest tested the temperature of the water with his foot. The priest poured the hot water, undressed, and was about to step into the water when a clear line of fire opened with the window. I took careful aim and rapidly fired three rounds into the side of the bathtub. The water drained through three holes. The priest stared at the three fountains of water and turned away silently. He did not moan or roar in anger. Gorgeous told the altar boys that the priest protested to federal agents that the sabotage of his bathtub was a crime against the Roman Catholic Church. The altar boys continued their priestly duties, of course, and never once uttered a word about the many torments. Bear, as usual, nailed a wooden cross above the window.

That Saturday, after five stations of torment, Shelter, my mother, was very worried about the violence on the reservation. She had no idea the altar boys were the sponsors of the priestly torments and that her son was the sniper. She prayed for the salvation of the priest and the Indian Mission Church of the Snow. Hail Mary, full of grace, the Lord is with thee.

Amen, Alleluia.

The Sixth Torment was centered on that sensual manuscript, the *Manabosho Curiosa*. The priest was aroused, as you know, by the stories of sex with animals, and he regularly read at night from the curiosa. Pants unlocked one of the high windows in the mission residence. At the right moment we could open the window from the outside. The position of the Fifth Torment, the bathtub scene, from the white pine was a true line of fire. The Fourth Torment, the outhouse, was an oblique shot, not a direct line of fire. I climbed a thick hemlock spruce closer to the mission and pushed aside branches for a clear view of the bed and nightstand. I raised my rifle as the priest slowly turned pages of the *Manabosho Curiosa*. He had marked several erotic scenes and must have turned to his favorite, fantasy sex with the white tailed deer, that night. I could see the turn of his facial expressions in the telescopic sight. He lightly touched his penis and then slowly masturbated as he read the story. I aimed directly at his erect penis, the rosy head, and considered for a moment the justice of a single sniper shot that night. I moved the sight to the manuscript, steady, between heartbeats, and fired one round through the open window. The bullet was precise and shredded the manuscript. Father Meme leaped out of bed and ran naked to the confessional. We brushed the snow to remove our footprints, as usual, but that night there was no need to hurry. The priest was at last struck by the sniper terror of the stations of torment. Bear placed a wooden cross by the window. The priest burned the cross in the morning.

The Seventh Torment was a rather easy maneuver, and the altar boys were more brazen and nervy because the priest was scared to death of the sniper. Gorgeous warned us that warriors are plucky but always cautious, and a sniper is never casual because it weakens his confidence and dedication. He was absolutely right, the altar boys were tempted to become daredevils once the priest was on the run. The seventh shot was through an open door early that morning. Father Meme always opened the door for breakfast. He was a creature of the winter, heartened by the cold. He rarely wore shoes in the mission residence. I focused the sight on a half loaf of hard bread and fired one round. The bread exploded on the table. The second shot shattered the butter dish. The priest cut his foot on a shard of glass as he rushed to the confessional. That was the first time his bloody footprint was not a from nose-bleed. Bear waited and then placed a wooden cross on the table. I am not entirely certain, *madame*, why the altar boys decided to place stained wooden crosses at each site of the torments, except to point to the obvious, the priest had burned the wooden grave markers of our ancestors, and the crosses were a fierce satire on the fourteen devotions of the Stations of the Cross.

The Eighth Torment was a truly nasty maneuver, *madame*, because the altar boys denied the priest his only sense of peace at the mission. That does not mean we hesitated for a minute. Actually, we were even more dedicated to terminate his sense of peace. Father Meme listened almost every night to the old time serial broadcasts on the radio in his station wagon. He could have listened to the shows in the mission residence, but for some reason his station wagon was a more secure refuge for his cowboy visions and adventures. The Lone Ranger was his favorite radio show. He actually bounced in the seat, *madame*, and the station wagon became a fantastic horse. The priest was revealed in his own western movie as he galloped away with the Lone Ranger and Tonto. Hi yo Silver, away. My target was the radio that night of the torments, the very heart of his favorite radio story. The position and sight were not as easy as a butter dish. Pants secretly opened a back window of the station wagon, and we measured the line of fire. I aimed at the dial light on the radio, waited for a signal from the altar boys, and then fired one round at the sound of the Lone Ranger. Father Meme could not hear the shot and thought the radio had lost power. The bullet struck one of the station keys and was hardly noticed that winter night. He started the engine to charge the battery. The radio was dead, sacrificed by a righteous sniper. The priest slumped over the steering wheel, and the station wagon moved as he wept. Bear hooked a wooden cross on the radio dials.

The Ninth Torment should have been easy, but the priest had enlisted at once several monks for protection and security. Father Meme was hesitant to contact the county sheriff or federal agents for fear that his priestly perversions would be exposed. Swayback posed as the counterpart of the secret service, vigilant to the risk of snipers. He was always with the priest, and three other unsavory monks moved into the mission residence. Saint John's Abbey became a safe place for seminarians by their absence. The altar boys watched the mission residence at a distance. The monks danced, shouted, laughed, and moaned in ecstasy. The altar boys were true warriors, and we waited for a chance to torment the priest that cold night. Finally, the priest opened the door, peered out, and then walked slowly toward the outhouse. Swayback was at his side, carrying a kerosene lantern. I waited in white camouflage near a red pine, concentrated on the steady motion of the lantern, and then fired one round at the rise of the light. The bullet shattered the mantle, but the wick held a flame. Swayback cried in panic, and the priest had a nosebleed that stained his nightshirt. They both ran back to the mission residence. The monk tripped on his shoelaces and tumbled into the deep snow. Bear placed a wooden cross next to the shattered lantern.

The Tenth Torment was much easier that the other nine. The priest ventured out to gather firewood that morning. He probably thought the sniper would not be around so early. The altar boys anticipated his many moods and moves, and we returned at dawn to surprise the priest with another torment. He gathered firewood for the cast iron stove. I focused the sight on the woodpile and rapidly fired several rounds. The bullets crashed into several split logs. The priest dropped the firewood, shouted to the monks, and bolted for the mission residence. Bear placed a wooden cross on the woodpile.

The Eleventh Torment was a straightforward but different maneuver, the crack of a snow shovel. Father Meme set out that afternoon with three security monks to shovel the path to the mission church. The heavy snow, more than a foot overnight, crowned gravestones, pine trees, and property. The altar boys returned from school and saw the priest with his bodyguards from the monkery. We decided to carry out the torment at once. Daylight maneuvers were uncertain and risky, but the new snow was a perfect cover for the maneuver. I decided to torment the priest at a great distance for a sniper. Far enough away that no one could ever incriminate the altar boys. Secretly we climbed onto the roof of the remote federal school. I could barely see the priest on the path near the mission. I set the inclination, wind direction, distance drop of the bullet, and focused the telescopic sight on the handle of the shovel. This was the most complicated and chancy shot of the torments. The shovel moved in my sight. I knew he would rest on the shovel every few minutes. The first round passed about two inches from the target. That was my first miss as a sniper, but the wind was not predictable at that distance. I moved the sight to the right and fired. The second round shattered the lower handle of the shovel. Father Meme shouted and waved the broken handle over his head, and the monks ran in three directions searching for the sniper. The distance was much too great for them to imagine that an altar boy was the sniper. I stored the rifle in a school closet, and we studied in the library for the next hour.

The Twelfth Torment was the next day on the north side of Wiindigoo Lake. The priest and monks decided to snowshoe around the lake, certain that the sniper was not ready for the deep snow. The altar boys were warriors, and we were forever prepared to outwit the wicked priest. We knew the rocks, creeks, trees, the rise and creases of the land around the lake, and we wore white camouflage. Bear watched the priest and monks snowshoe to the north, around the lake, and then we set out in the other direction to create a scene of winter torment. Nishiwe was at home. Gray smoke was rising from the chimney of his cabin, but we did not want to share the strategies of our twelfth maneuver. Sneeze walked close to my side, and we were both worried about the four cabin mongrels. The snow was soft, hardly a sound by snowshoe to the granite rocks near the lake. We could hear the monks in the distance. Swayback teased the priest about his nickname, surely a reference to his rosy penis. The loud laughter of the monks ruined the natural scenes. I cleared a position in a hollow of a boulder, with a view of the path near the lake. The altar boys brushed the snow with pine boughs to remove any trace of our presence. The priest was weary and dragged his heavy trail snowshoes. I concentrated on the sound of their voices, pictured the pace and motion of the priest, and braced the rifle on the boulder for a steady sight and shot. The position was perfect. The priest and monks had to turn to the west near the massive boulder, at that point the trail snowshoes would be a clear target. I moved the sight with the priest, a slow, steady pace, and fired two rounds at the points of the trail snowshoes. The bullets were accurate and cracked the pointed birch toes of the snowshoes. The tight rawhide moose webbing unraveled, and the priest toppled over in the snow. Swayback thought the priest had been shot, but the blood on the snow was only a nosebleed. The priest tried to stop the bleeding with the sleeve of his coat. The monks gathered around the priest and cursed the sniper in every direction. The ravens circled and croaked at the noisy clergy. Swayback and the priest were scared of ravens. The monastic band trudged through the snow, but the priest was exhausted. Swayback noticed smoke in the distance, and soon the monks were at the cabin. Nishiwe sent the mongrels out to corner the monks. Then he came out and told the monks to pray for nature and his mongrels. The monks shouted at the old man that a sniper shot the mission priest. The altar boys were nearby. I heard the monk and worried that my second shot might have wounded the priest. The monk told a lie to protect the priest. Nishiwe set out with his mongrels to find the priest. Father Meme was covered with blood, but his only wounds were virtue and morality. The ravens circled, and the mongrels backed away from the priest. Most dogs are curious about the scent of blood, but not the blood of a perverse priest. Nishiwe invited the priest into his cabin and prepared some herbal tea to cure his nosebleeds. The priest refused to drink the tea. Nishiwe told my great uncle that the monks noticed the gun cabinet in the corner and suspected he was the sniper. Swayback asked the old man if he was the sniper. Nishiwe stared at the monks in silence. He locked the gun cabinet, and then walked out of his own cabin to avoid the monks. The mongrels snarled and chased the priest and monks back to the path around Wiindigoo Lake. Sneeze remained at my side, buried in the snow. Bear later that night tied a wooden cross on the snowshoes stacked near the mission residence.

The Thirteenth Torment was carried out in only a few seconds' time. The priest wore a high black hat at most church activities, if only to cover his tangled mound of red hair. I knew he would leave early that morning in his hat. I centered the sight on the station wagon. I fired one round at the very top of his hat as he paused to open the door of the station wagon. The bullet knocked his hat into the snow. He stood in silence by the door, looked down, and then turned to recover his hat. The priest pushed a finger through two holes near the crown and waved the hat over his head, a gesture to the mysterious sniper. He sat in the station wagon for a few minutes and then drove away. Bear later tied a wooden cross to the rearview mirror.

The Fourteenth Torment, the last torment, was quite random compared to the previous thirteen maneuvers. The altar boys decided that at least one of the maneuvers should include in some way the bloody nose episodes of the priest. We were not certain, however, how a sniper could scare the priest over his recurrent nosebleeds. I sat in the white pine for several hours waiting for the priest to leave the mission residence. The last torment would be no more than chance. Pants told me later the priest was listening to a native woman in the nave, who wanted to work at the mission, when his nose started to bleed. He rushed into the confessional for a cache of towels to absorb the blood. Shortly after the woman confessed her sins to the priest, he carried the bloody mound of towels to the outhouse. I moved my sight to the bundle of towels, but a shot then might have been deadly. The line of fire was open, however, when he reached the outhouse. I fired one round at the bloody bundle. The bullet tore the towels from his hand. He turned and ran back to the mission residence. Bear nailed the second and last wooden cross on the outhouse.

Father Meme was truly scared and distracted by the sniper, but he would never be shamed or burdened by guilt for his sexual perversions and depravity. He revealed no humor, no play or native sense of irony. The priest never informed or complained to the police about the sniper. Any formal scrutiny of a crime might have revealed his corruption and surely turned into a more serious torment than the sniper. The Fourteen Torments were a nuisance to the priest but never a serious moral concern, and he continued with his obsessive, sleazy, sexual practices. He persistently pursued and tried to seduce the altar boys, unaware that we were the instant cause of his daily torments.

Swayback and the other monks stayed at the mission for a week after the sniper scares and then returned to the Monastic Residence at Saint John's Abbey. Father Meme once again, *madame*, was so needy for sex with the altar boys that he was easily lured to the fish house. The fourteen sniper torments had ended three weeks earlier, and the priest was even more confident about his seduction of the altar boys. Months earlier we had decided the priest must be shamed and sacrificed, so we abandoned him to the mosquitoes on Namakan Island. Barba, as you know, persuaded the altar boys to rescue the priest and monk. Father Meme was wary for a time, but soon returned to his sexual abuses at the mission. The Fourteen Torments denied the priest any sense of peace for three weeks, but he was immutable, unashamed, and continued his unnatural breach of celibacy. He molested our honor, trust, and bodies. That Friday, March 12, 1954, more than thirteen centuries since the death of Saint Gregory the Great, we sacrificed the wicked priest in the fish house. Father Meme was never a man of truth or beauty, not even by steady confessions or forgiveness. His mere breath left a terrible stain in memory. These are the perceptions of the priest that last, the absence of nature and beauty.

Saint Gregory, as you know, *madame*, survived famine, pestilence, and the vicious, gruesome, sexual abuses of barbarians in the sixth century. He was a dedicated healer and lived by reverence, care, and the sacred trust of meditation. Later he created a godly discourse and established monasteries in Sicily and Rome. Pope Gregory was elected by unanimous consent and served for fourteen years until his death on March 12, 604. Pope Gregory and Father Conan Whitty died on the same calendar day. The altar boys were convinced that the sacrifice of a sexual predator, the demoniac priest, was inspired by a divine contrary, the consecrated presence and death of Saint Gregory. Native visions and the natural reason of contraries, the enemy way, trickster stories, animal conversions, and transmutations create a sense of eternal presence. Contraries tease and cure the heart by humor and irony, but the penis predators wound memory. The mission priest was denounced by stories of resistance, overcome by native ingenuity and the exercise of survivance over victimry. The absolutes of monotheism never were the natural sources of native reason and futurity.

The altar boys waited for the priest at the altar rail. I sounded the sacred bells and poured the sacramental wine. Father Meme blessed a child with webbed fingers and then prayed for the polio vaccine, the hydrogen bomb test at Eniwetok Atoll in the Pacific, and the health of President Eisenhower. There were seven parishioners and two visitors at the service that morning. The visitors to the mission church might have thought the priest was enlightened to mention the nuclear arms race on a reservation. How would the parishioners and visitors ever know, *madame*, that the priest sexually abused the altar boys? Sunday Mass was the last time we would serve the priest and the last time he would celebrate Holy Communion at the Indian Mission Church of the Snow. The altar boys sacrificed the priest five days later.

Father Meme rushed to the fish house at twilight, enticed by the devious invitation of the altar boys. Pants told the priest we wanted to masturbate with him over the fish hole. The altar boys waited for the priest to light the kerosene lantern. Truly, *madame*, we waited because we were scared. The decision to sacrifice the priest, after fourteen days of torments, was obviously much easier than to actually carry out the brutal action. I might have shot the priest as a sniper, but the deceit of sex with the altar boys was worrisome. Bear was the first to make a move, and so we gathered our beaver and lilac coups sticks for the sacrifice. There was time to turn back, but the closer we came to the fish house that night the more determined we were to torture the priest to death. We stood by the two wooden crosses on the door and listened to his heavy breath inside the cold fish house, the haunted sexual moan of the priest. I was the first to enter and face the sacrifice. The priest was nude, seated on a bench near the fish hole. His thighs were spread wide open, and the skin was rosy. He had already started to masturbate. The priest reached out to touch my penis, hesitated, and then hurried me to remove my clothes. The scent of his pungent body filled the fish house. The altar boys arrived with a bundle of sticks, *madame*, and the priest never seemed to notice. Bear untied the sticks and leaned each weapon against the bench. Three of the sticks were birch cut by beaver at Namakan Island. The other sticks were lilac, narrow, curved, strong, and pliable. Pants turned away when the priest touched his penis. Father Meme was so obsessed about sex with three altar boys that he could not fully understand the situation, the first scene of a fish house scourge. Bear raised a lilac stick over his head and then beat the priest on the shoulders. The priest flinched, but he was not surprised, and did not seem to feel any pain. I beat the priest on the back with a thick, birch beaver stick. Pants whipped the priest on the chest and thighs with two lilac sticks. I cried and shouted at the priest that his abuse shamed the altar boys. I denounced him as a sex criminal. The priest looked away and never responded. Pants demanded the priest show some sign of shame and remorse for his crimes. Bear beat the priest on the neck and back and shouted that he should crave clemency, mercy, and forgiveness from the altar boys. The altar boys condemned the priest with each beat of the sticks. Father Meme was incapable of sorrow and would never reveal shame or contrition. I was worried because the priest seemed to be aroused by the beating. The pain became a pleasure. His body was marked but not yet bloody.

The altar boys beat the priest for more than an hour. His body was swollen, and blood oozed from the wounds. The priest actually leaned into the sticks and never tried to block the beating. He was aroused and masturbated even more vigorously. The altar boys backed away, aghast at the bloody body of the priest slumped over the bench. The sticks were bloody, the bench was bloody, the hands of the altar boys were bloody, and the entire fish house was bloody. The priest continued to masturbate in silence. Slow, unsteady, bloody finger strokes of his penis. I could not hear his breath, but he moved his icy eyes and hands.

Please, *madame*, forgive these brutal, grievous scenes in my story, a sudden rush from heartfelt memories. I must try to create a narrative of the sacrifice. I swear, the priest had turned the pain of torture into a perverse pleasure. Only his nose was not bloody. Pants cried as he beat the priest on the head with a thick beaver stick. The priest turned to face the stick. His face was already swollen, lips cracked. Suddenly the priest leaned over and ejaculated into the fish hole. The altar boys were sick and disgusted by the spectacle. Father Meme turned, smiled faintly, and then closed his eyes. Blood ran down his cheeks, chest, and crotch. The priest was silent and never uttered a word as he was beaten for more than an hour. The sound of his mushy, bloody flesh is forever in my memory. I was silent, shamed by my own violence. Bear tried to push the hefty bloody body into the fish hole. The corpse of the priest was cold, slimed with blood, and too massive to slide through the hole in the ice.

The altar boys estimated the breadth of the dead priest and chopped the ice to enlarge the hole. We pushed and pushed the priest head first into the ice hole, and his breath bubbled in the cold water. He was alive, *madame*, and his miserable, slow death, the unsteady, lingering breath, lasted for more than an hour. The fish hole had to be widened twice more to accommodate the corpse. Finally the faint breath bubbles stopped, and the altar boys pushed the whole bloody body of the priest through the hole into the cold water. The corpse moved under the ice, turned slowly, his huge teeth exposed by a wide sinister smile. The last image we remembered that night was the white face and red hair of the priest pressed against the underside of the thick ice. The altar boys, *ma chère madame*, sacrificed much more than the wicked priest that winter night at Wiindigoo Lake.